CW00664694

WINTER
ANIMALS

WINTER ANIMALS

ASHANI LEWIS

dialogue
books

DIALOGUE BOOKS

First published in Great Britain in 2024 by Dialogue Books

10 9 8 7 6 5 4 3 2 1

A CIP catalogue record for this book
is available from the British Library.

Hardback ISBN 978-0-349-70329-9
C-format ISBN 978-0-349-70330-5

Typeset in Berling by M Rules
Printed and bound in Great Britain by
Clays Ltd, Elcograf S.p.A

Papers used by Dialogue Books are from well-managed forests
and other responsible sources.

Dialogue Books
Carmelite House
50 Victoria Embankment
London EC4Y 0DZ

www.dialoguebooks.co.uk

Dialogue Books, part of Little, Brown, Book Group Limited,
an Hachette UK company.

This book is dedicated to my father.

Chapter 1

The brewery sits under the mountains in the part of Bend, Oregon where the town turns to high desert. Yoghurt shops and hardware stores dissolve, first into heathery stretches of far-apart houses and then into emptier, rockier land. High Desert RV Services is the last stop before the steppe. Miles of road, gorse and telephone wire; junco sparrows in the winter. There is snow in the Cascades to the west, even in the summer, invisibly blue. Snow is still falling in Bend proper, late into the year. It is falling thinly, it touches the gorse in the desert. The brewery is in the process of upscaling.

Elen, thirty-eight and on her third dark beer, watches the door opening onto the whited airless drift. Teenagers, two boys and two girls. She returns to the beer but they're hard to ignore; not one has wiped their feet and hulls of snow in the shape of toecaps follow them to their chairs, disappearing slowly. What's the vernacular of dispossession? Snow is a part of it. Tonight, the beer also helps dissolve the image of once-owned things, but snow takes her footprints out of the dirt in her old driveway; in thick banks it buries the skip outside a house that was once hers.

*

The teenagers are shiny and chattering, fresh from the slopes. They collect around the bar; they roll cigarettes, they might be British. Between Elen and the four teenagers is the gentle relatedness which exists between the only customers in an empty brewhouse, and so she's uncomfortable but not startled when they approach her booth with five beers.

'Drinks for the house,' jokes a short, tanned boy who Elen will come to think of as the main one, and then, bright-eyed, 'Do you mind if we sit with you?'

Elen shakes her head, takes the drink. The teenagers are, in fact, all a few years clear of the same English university. The main one is called Luka. There's Clover, beautiful, whose 'no-spend year after uni was, just, epiphanic', and George, cigarette behind each ear, utterly changed after 'doing India'. ('We did India together,' says Luka, and Elen wonders for a moment if India is another Clarins-shiny one of them.)

Lyn is slightly cooler to Elen than the rest. She sits a little way apart and sends looks to Luka as if she's not sure what they're doing in the booth. Thin, blonde, perfect. Her eyes are clear without being friendly. Elen finds herself hoping they cannot tell she's thirty-eight.

They call themselves squatters. They had graduated from using Airbnb to cruise empty homes during their periods of vacancy, always in ski areas and always with intention to ski ('That's how we did Hintertux'). The parents all thought they were staying at lodges, but it was actually Luka's father who had put them on to the fact that this entire complex had been abandoned. He did something in property, Luka told her vaguely.

'What do you do?' he asks her, finally. Elen pauses and the beer begins a new wash of her insides.

'I was a wife.' Elen's ex-husband had been a vault teller in a bank. They had lived in Bend for more than fifteen years. Two months after he left, she had been given notice on the house. This morning, she returned from the Post Office to find that the locks were changed and her landlord had blocked her number. Elen retrieved what she could from the skip outside the house. Some things she put in the back of her car; most had been taken for rubble by snow. 'It's fine,' she finishes. 'I'm driving to Michigan tomorrow. I'll stay there for a while.' She doesn't say with her parents, or think too hard about three nights of sleeping in her car. There was no way to reconcile – least of all to these healthy, disinterested faces – the homemaker she had been with what was left; the bar, the car, the beer, the snow.

There's a small white quiet, after which Luka manages a nonplussed 'Michigan. Very cool.'

Elen has a pale little mouth which used to be pretty; she's allergic to fish, and looks it. Deep in the booth with the teenagers, she begins to feel dark and shrewd. Their voices are painfully British, clipped, sometimes childish. They invite her to stay with them, and she accepts.

They take her towards the mountains. Elen's inclined to think that she's made a mistake, not because of the long drive into the lonely dark of the Cascades Lakes Byway where bones gleam and snow puddles on the sides of the road, but because the manic, inaccessible patter with which they fill her silences has not yet let up. She's relieved when the car stops.

The resort complex had been abandoned going on five years. Clover tells her there had been an accident, the death of a young man skiing backcountry, after which the resort had shut down. Elen corrects her: the resort had been built for a series of competitions which were now over, the ski club running them had dissolved and the premises fallen into simple, ghostless, disuse.

Lyn unloads some more things from the car into the designated girls' room: extra blankets, a third sleeping mat for Elen. ('That's lucky,' she says, nodding at the mat. 'You never know when you're going to make a friend,' says Luka.) There is a long dorm-wide mirror, fly-spotted. On the table beneath, Lyn and Clover have laid out their balms. Sun lotion, cold cream. Two silver lipsticks. The teenagers exude belonging, move around the resort like they were born to it.

That these children should have wound up in Bend the day before she was due to leave is a neat coincidence. They're occupying spaces that she has already committed to memory. Not the mountain so much; she hasn't skied in a few years – certainly, she has no more real claim than them to an empty resort which she had never visited. Except that, at the very least, it's a half hour drive from the fifteen years of living in Bend that she has already beerily ceded.

In the daytime, the canteen had been the eeriest part; the spectre of a functioning resort moved most clearly here where the cutlery had been left unpacked and there were tannin stains still on the coffee cups. It was a kinder place in the evening. The boys had cooked – porcini risotto over a camping stove – and the whole hall now smelled of food and use. Instead of cold slope-side daylight, one battery lantern shone from under a cotton scarf, another from behind a bottle of white wine; the light from both diffusing soft and gently coloured. They sit on the floor to eat and the light moves on the walls like the sea. Elen feels calm and separate.

This is what it's all about, Luka tells her, this is why they do what they do, a slow-cooked meal at the end of the ski day; it's sustainable living, it's something closer to real life, something that elevates their real life. 'It's anti-seasonaire. Alpine living, not just skiing spliced with Jägermeister and Europop.' He catches himself. 'Why am I telling you about alpine living, right?'

Elen smiles obediently at her luck. As the meal falls warm apart in her stomach, she thinks that she has lived for a while now without any of this charm – moisturisers in their little pots, risotto, soft light: the adorable hallmarks of a thoughtless life.

In the morning they kit her out. Half of it is put together from Clover's spares; the jacket is George's and there are skis piled high in a room with a broken lock that feels like a bunker. Lyn shows her stoically to a part of the reception where dozens of ski boots have sat in boxes collecting dust.

'Do you think someone is coming back for these?'

'Not for a while.'

'Have you always skied?'

Lyn exhales. The snow – blue, invisible; the gorse, cold in the desert. 'Yeah. Since I was very young. My dad and

George's dad actually used to take us skiing together. Like, all of my friends do spin classes now, I just think this is much better. It's kind of like getting back to the land.' She is wearing a blue angora mix under her Moncler. The moon is still up. Outside, the mountain looms and obliterates.

The nearest chairlift is miles from their route, so the whole day is composed of climbs for hours for descents over in minutes. They make the climbs in twos and threes; they talk, George smokes. The sky is Pacific.

The first descent is over too soon. Initially, Elen concentrates on not falling, overworking her eyes scanning the slopes for their hidden jags and divots. Something slides, and then she is going for the first time in years. She moves so fast through the air and so smooth over the land and she doesn't want to make a metaphor of anything but she is on the edge of a real thought, all cold and whistling and whitely gliding, and it is that she is a transcendent impulse housed in a body. After, she feels it all through, under her tongue and between her legs, and she isn't thinking of Michigan the whole way.

Elen makes the next ascent with George and Clover. 'I used to smoke up before skiing,' says George, describing a joint with his hands. 'But these guys are purists.' Clover looks at him. 'And they're right!'

'You're so lucky to have grown up around a mountain like this,' says Clover. 'To really know it.' (Elen gets the sense she's being paid some kind of homage, and does not explain that she grew up in Michigan.) 'I guess you're sorry to be leaving.'

She is looking up at Elen, blithe, lovely, naturally over-collagenous. Even though the painted nightstand that she'd kept her paracetamols in for ten years is in a skip, or possibly now a landfill, Elen does not shake her. Instead, she says, 'It used to be a volcano. Might still be.'

There were other things she could and should have told Clover. She'd done a form of growing up there. It was hers. There were things she knew. Mirror Pond in the fall and the names of little children in her part of town. She didn't expect that little children occurred to people like Lyn and Clover. Once, the city had only been a point on a river that the pioneers called the Farewell Bend, the last point before you couldn't look back. Once, she had wanted to live in a mountain town because she liked mountains. Perennials and alpine plants growing star shaped. The air, colder, thinner, run through with birds; mountain roses in the backyard where she could take her coffee. And through the windows of the green-lined café where she would have breakfast and watch no one come and no one go, the crags going chalky in the sun. She had wanted to live in a desert town – beers, she imagined, at a gas station with the sun overhead and then nothing else for miles – because she liked deserts.

On the left, Lyn twists down the slope like a blonde sheet of ice. Easy grace. When they switch routes, she doubles down on the quick turns, sends snow spray back up the mountain in staggered powder. Volcano, still; sleeping enormity, atavistic and underneath her. Elen knows they are the better skiers, but old things in her legs are waking up.

Chapter 2

It was possible to forget from the Cascades that Bend was not all spare and gleaming. It was not the homogenous purity of mountain and high desert. It was one of *Men's Journal*'s '10 Best Places to Live Now': a small but growing city, encumbered by civilisation like anywhere else. There was a tanned, sunglasses-wearing imperative to throw yourself into all Bend had to offer, lakes and peaks and trails; there was an energy among its denizens, a vigour that could be described as infectious or, less kindly, as cultish. The bumper stickers read *Your vacation is our life*; it was all a lot of pressure. Elen had not thrown herself into it, so to speak. She hadn't gone body boarding every Saturday morning; she hadn't really liked to jog. Robert hadn't either, but at least he'd wished that he had. She'd liked it best in the fall when the tourists faded off. Leaves rushing or floating on the surfaces of things. They gravitated more to each other when the cold pressed in at their house, exchanged small survivalist touches more frequently.

Robert's brother and his wife were very much body-boarding types. They hiked; they were community spirited. She was on the Fish Passage Advisory Panel, a committee that had spent seven years trying to fund a 'fish ladder' so that certain endangered fishes could pass through the obstructed Mirror Pond as part of their natural migrations. (Seven years. How expensive could a fish ladder be?) Everyone should have a hobby that they couldn't put on their CV, Robert's brother had instructed Elen once. She'd been out of the game for a while, but she was quite sure that white-water rafting or whatever remained CV appropriate. Still, it was sweet, she supposed: they went out of their way to include her in things. That's how she'd become involved in the quail egg business.

The two months after Robert left, Elen spent a lot of time looking back and found she couldn't believe how many of her married memories revolved around the quail eggs. There were three farmer's markets in Bend; it was quite a business, though she barely saw the money. Her brother-in-law and his wife, Susannah, kept nearly twenty quails in their front room. They lived in two 'hotels': tall, multi-level hutches raised off the ground, the males in the smaller tower. The little boy liked to run around with them. Sometimes he would try to take one to bed. Elen tucked him in on occasion, and would have to alert his parents to the small chirps from underneath his duvet. He was a real angel, her nephew, though his parents were busybodies. She and Susannah would sit packing eggs in cartons of six. They were like dollhouse eggs; there was a little doll-sized quail on the packaging in the corner of the label. 'You're so good with Lee.' (Pause, pick a feather off.) Robert and his brother were very close. She felt that Susannah knew things about their marriage that she herself didn't. Do you think something's lacking, Susannah had asked. She hadn't said a child, but Elen had felt herself about ready to put a thumb straight through the eggshell.

The quails caused arguments about money. She was wasting time with other people's work. There would be shouting and upset and cold, but then she would say, *We're talking about quails, Robert.* And they would laugh hysterically at the brother-in-law, and sit on the couch together and be close . . .

Their arguments were all similar: some about quails, some about dinner, some about how she didn't do much but keep house for two people. It was more involved than that though, because there was a space in the garden which they let to tourists. A standalone room with a view of the Cascades, rentable a night at a time: a tiny shed which blocked the sunlight from the camas and the blue-eyed grass. Elen was in charge of the room, and of giving the guests a breakfast, although Robert was in charge more broadly of all their money.

She didn't love the guests, but she loved the house, she did. She knew the origin of everything in it. It was the opposite feeling to when you grow up and everything in your home seems autochthonous, sprung from the walls, born on those shelves, but it was an equally lovely feeling, one of closeness. Elen could walk past a table and name the street where each item upon it had been bought or found. Often they'd been found: when she and Robert had first furnished the house fifteen years ago, they'd picked up some lovely pieces left outside people's houses. A stream of good luck, a blessing. One nightstand, antique, painted – very beautiful. They'd carried it home from outside a big ski lodge in a less populated outskirt of Bend.

*

But then the house became simply the place they argued every day. Just about little things, the tone of her voice. You think it's no work, keeping house for two people. But it's work, and work. It's work to get up sometimes. At its worst, he would FaceTime her from one room while she was in another. To tell her to please be sweet to him, or that he didn't see why he should have to look at her today.

There was a woman at the bank that she'd thought Robert might find sexy. She alternated between feeling sick about it and not caring. The woman was popular, social, didn't spend time packaging quails' eggs with her sister-in-law. Elen wondered about the tendency to find attractive those people who were easy with others and made friends quickly, if it was an evolutionarily sexy thing. She tried to find one of the men who'd come to stay attractive, a big guy from Texas who looked funny sleeping in their little guesthouse. He and a friend had planned to sleep on the beach, but it wasn't quite summer and he'd decided he couldn't hack it. This had revolted her. Robert had asked if she thought the Texan was sexy. She'd told him that she did. They'd had energetic sex that night but then not again for weeks.

For three years her drinking had slowly increased. In the last couple Elen's drinking had her dehydrated very often, which in Oregon meant that most months she couldn't walk down the street without the sun diamonding migraines at her. She wove through tourists with her eyes shut, got lost in knots of them clustering to see the last Blockbuster in existence. Robert never mentioned it; it occurred to her that he liked her better this way. Sometimes they had friendly nights – he'd be drinking as well, they'd get on, dance in the kitchen, fall asleep in front of the TV. But the friendly nights made the nights that she drank by herself worse. They made it clearer that these nights were comprised of a different kind of drinking: vodka in a mug and the same sad illicitness as when she'd been fifteen and getting her rocks off to Wendy Botha's *Playboy* spread. Then she stopped hiding it in mugs. She could finish twelve cans of beer in a night and all the while Robert would be sat at his laptop ignoring her and she'd be looking out into their slightly scrubby garden and wondering.

That vista is pretty fixed in her memory: their garden, buckling slightly from the beers. There were fairy lights in a trellis configuration down one side of the tiny 'guesthouse'. They'd been a gift from Susannah, ages ago, and they were still bright. When Elen and Robert had first come up with the idea of keeping guests, it had been a new lease of life; it plugged the two of them together into the Bend ethos, had them rubbing elbows with its energising pilgrims without preventing them from laughing at tourist behaviour. But it was just another thing on the calendar now. The fairy lights would be twinkling camply, some stranger would be disrobing in their shed. Just behind, oh my god the mountain. The mountain was never out of sight. From Elen's kitchen window, it looked like it sprang out of the foot of their garden. The various *it's so beautifuls* from guests meant very little to her, until the big Texan was marvelling at its blue faces. That was fantastic. His hand next to her wrist on the porch rail, snow in its white lines distinguishing rock from shadow miles away. She could feel Robert watching as the Texan waved his fingers

to indicate how the clouds parted for the rounded summit –
she felt excited, desired. Less than a week later she was back
to not caring about desire. Robert tried to nestle in the night
and she moved over.

So he left. 'Left' was euphemistic. He had vanished in the
night. Had it been the night? That period is slightly blurry
for her, not so much because of the drinking as because every
day was identical. After Robert went, Elen cancelled the
remaining Airbnb appointments. She stayed in, some days
drinking, some days not, with little difference. Bend seemed
overbright, and shriekingly loud with birds and tourists. On
one of the days there came a knock at the door. Elen wasn't
chain smoking under the bedclothes but she'd been lying on
the sofa for three hours. She had turned on her side a while
ago and not moved since, just laid staring in the direction of
the television, which was off. The knock came again, firmer.
It was within her rights not to answer. If it was important they
would have called first. Though she hadn't been looking at
her phone. Someone called her name through the letterbox.
'Let us in.'

It was Susannah. Elen refocused her eyes and, with silent
effort, rose. Susannah continued to call in the twenty seconds
it took to pull a pair of sweatpants on and Elen rethought
letting her in, but did it anyway. Susannah wasn't someone
who would go away on her own.

'Oh, Elen.'

With horror, Elen realised that her sister-in-law was not
alone. Lee held her hand; he smiled unselfconsciously at
Elen from somewhere around hip height. Susannah pushed

through into the house. Elen hadn't even thought to stand in her way.

'How are you doing?'

'I'm fine.' The voice came from Elen's mouth; she was occupied with Lee. There were cars and things somewhere that he liked to play with. She didn't know where they were now.

Susannah sat, began to fend off questions Elen hadn't fathomed asking. They'd had no idea that Robert was thinking of leaving – no idea things had been that bad – no idea where he was now. But they were here now, they (she) wanted to support Elen as much as was possible.

'I'm fine,' Elen said again, absently. She'd wanted help, or company, in the week before; she'd mouthed quietly her desire for it into the sheets. But now she just wanted them out of this house. She would have a bath when they were gone, a long bath and a cold beer.

Susannah wanted to know what she was going to do. Elen sighed, watched Lee peel a brown strip of leatherette off the arm of the sofa without attempting to stop him. It was good that he had the pleasure instinct anyway.

'Have you thought about ... have you spoken to Robert about making provisions for you?'

'I don't know ...'

'Elen, I know it's hard. But the house—'

With effort again, she finished the sentence. 'I don't know ... where the fuck he is, Susannah.' It was pleasing, and true, so she said it again. 'I don't know where the fuck he is. I don't know where the fuck he is. How the fuck can I talk to a man about money when I don't know where the fuck he is?'

Susannah looked away. She didn't say anything for a

minute, just plucked Lee's finger out of the sofa's soft innards, and then stood up. 'We'll talk when you're feeling better. But really, anything we can do. We're here, both of us.' She lowered her voice. 'You mustn't just stay in drinking, sweetheart.'

'Bye Auntie Elen,' said Lee, pulled backwards out of the house.

Elen nodded, still blank in the face, still ringing in the stomach with the truth of not knowing where the fuck he was. Susannah was right, she couldn't just stay in drinking. She took a bath and went out to drink.

And so, finally out of the house, Elen had crossed paths with the teenagers a couple of times before they met in the brewery. For the few weeks before, they had been rushing Bend like a four-person army. It was for them predominantly wonder, amazement, joy! They shot through the crowds at the last Blockbuster with their eyes on the sky, mountains, North America. Their squatting season had started in Cerro Castor the year before, and had involved camping for weeks before they found empty a kind of reinforced yurt, once designated for glamping. Since then they'd skied around Europe, which had seemed awfully familiar in comparison. It was time to feel glossy and alien again and Bend was very, very blue.

George and Clover had gone rafting, crashing down the Deschutes River as Elen crossed a footbridge over it in what they would later identify as a slapstick near-miss; Lyn and Luka had only skied; they all regrouped to buy groceries for the week at the Whole Foods. The teenagers glided around like flat performances, their movements boundless; if it wasn't for the code of Happiness & Vigour in Bend, a couple of people might have hated them. They'd eaten out one day and made friends with a faction of Californians, who'd been glossy in a different way: long, tanned women in lip-gloss with UV protection and men with gunmetal necklaces and mirrored aviators. The Californians had all loved the teen-agers, the old Oxonian vibe, the story into which they could spin this meet. They'd loved it when Luka told them about the abandoned resort and invited them to stay, though of course they'd declined.

'What do you do?' the Californian in the brightest shirt had asked.

'We ski.'

'Love it,' he'd said. 'We're content producers. Yeah, full time.'

Luka had smiled hugely back at him. George was flirting with one, Lyn was taking care of accounts; Elen passed the restaurant on her way back from Walmart.

Elen, however, was beginning to find Bend full of overfamil-iar faces. Her friends were all shallow acquaintances, really. They were friends of Susannah's. But she had a few if she counted every woman she'd known from beer gardens and hiking trails when she first got to Bend who still stopped to talk when they met in the street, and she found that she could no longer stop to talk.

So: she followed her old egg route to the farmers' market furthest out and then she kept driving, drove past High Desert RV. She'd have to fill the tank before Michigan anyway. She drove further, drove to the brewery which was remote enough that it looked like the kind of place where a shoot-out might happen. The mountain is huge and histories collect under it. Bend was a crossing point before it was a settlement before it was a logging town before it was an outdoor-sports destination, but everywhere's always only a crossing point. That's where they found her.

Chapter 3

'That was gorgeous, huh?'

One of the teenagers aims this directly at her on the car ride back, after that first run on Mount Bachelor which has woken up old joists in her legs. Elen would love to be silent and lay her head against the rackety window and stare out at the Scenic Byway the whole way back but she can't deny that it was gorgeous. She says so. She's thinking again about how she's going to get to Michigan.

She thinks about Michigan for the rest of the evening and the light from the battery lanterns moves on the canteen walls like water through film. Her parents had moved a couple of towns over from the one she grew up in, but very similar: predominantly white, big moons in the lake, considerable wealth disparity. Her parents live in a small two-bedroom house; the guest bedroom is a child's bedroom but not her childhood bedroom and with none of her things in it, which Elen guesses is a reprieve. She's always hated the thing of spending a night in one's childhood bedroom – the familiar ceiling, the feeling that the length of the night is equivalent to all the thousands of nights you've ever spent there, laid out back-to-back.

Elen's mother is a bustler. She's awkward when they're in a room together alone; she scuttles. Elen's father's much friendlier, but this is from a place of natural friendliness rather than familial closeness. Elen is in the habit of almost never visiting; she knows that she puts them out when she comes to stay. They love their own space, love each other's company, though she can't imagine what they talk about. They hadn't loved Robert. They hadn't hated him, but on those rare visitations they had strange civilised disputes with him about things on which Elen had never before heard them express an opinion. Global warming and whatnot. Her father had the disputes; her mother bustled. And they saw Bend as an opt-out place for hipsters and tree-huggers, like Elen hadn't joined the real world, and they didn't mind at all that she hadn't had kids with Robert. Neither did Robert. Elen didn't mind that she hadn't had kids either, but god, was she the only woman in North America with a womb that no one had a real opinion on at all?

Her mother had had her when she was nearly forty. Later, when it had all happened, Elen would feel a pang for Michigan and the childhood-bedroom healing she could have had, though it was not her childhood bedroom. Tonight she goes to sleep thinking about Michigan, Clover making snuffling sounds into the sleeping mat next to her.

The next day feels like a repeat of a dream. They ski. It's bright, she's better, brief euphoria. And then, back in the haunted resort: the ache, the used-up muscles, the sounding out of a body. Everything you might want after a mountain day is unavailable, there is no warm bed, there is no hot bath.

The teenagers' improvised comforts are unfamiliar, off-brand, British versions of Elen's own home comforts. They torrent English television on a laptop connected to a power bank, panel shows with identical casts and almost no jokes. ('I think it's sad they never ask capital questions on *University Challenge,*' says George, who'd learned all the capital cities by heart at a young age, even the really difficult ones.) Clover makes them hot drinks which she prepares on the camp stove like a crazy person in response to the deprival of her no-spend year, total extravagance, piling them high like the Ned Flanders hot chocolate with mini marshmallows and whipped cream and cacao nibs from an organic store in Bend.

All this is asinine except for the rock face open like a wound out the window and Lyn's legs thrown immaculate over Clover's shoulders. It's how a college common room would be, she imagines. Elen removes herself – four people can't fit comfortably round a netbook anyway – and pretends to explore the hallways of the resort.

There are something like fifty bedrooms, all locked. The teak panels of the reception desk look warm and ancient. Some kind of weed has started leaking into the resort via the front door, sprawling over scuffed walls and springing up between tiles until it stops, affronted, at the potted skeleton of what might once have been an aspidistra. Elen considers taking a nap. She walks heavily through the halls to the girls' room. The problem with women was that Elen was always worried they were mocking her. When she was fifteen, a girl in the year above her had been making conversation in the lunch queue. 'Do you ever get hairs on your chin, Elen? Because I get hairs on my chin and I'm not sure what to do about them. If I pluck them, they'll just grow back thicker. And if not thicker, then darker, which gives the impression of thickness.' The girl had tapped her chin with long fingernails. Elen hadn't been able to see the hairs, but she hadn't doubted that they were there.

'I don't get hairs on my chin,' Elen had said. And then, willing to help: 'But I have kind of soft ones on the sides of my face, because of this new face cream. But I don't need to get rid of them because they're pretty fair. Listen, Marilyn Monroe had lots of little facial hairs and she refused to get rid of them because she thought they made her face softer on camera.' The girl had nodded and been promptly swallowed by the vortex of the lunchroom and memory. But for months afterwards Elen had wondered if she actually did have long dark hairs on her chin, and if this other girl had set her up. How stupid to be talking about Marilyn Monroe and the fair soft hairs on her cheek when she had whiskers! Elen sits heavily down in the girls' room: her mess of blankets and the shelled warmth of the other girls, nylon-ripstop, Mountain Hardwear brand. She will have to go back tomorrow; she will drive for days and she will reconstruct a life, something appropriate for a thirty-eight year old.

Like a conscientious squatter, Luka has driven some miles away to dump their waste in a garbage bin by the river. 'I've had a fucking lovely drive,' he calls down the corridor. 'Have you seen the state of that sunset? I think we should go for a walk.'

He nearly knocks Elen over when he turns the corner.

'Sorry!' He beams at her. 'You'd come for a walk, wouldn't you Elen?'

'I might start to pack up.' They both know there's no packing up to do; none of her things ever left the car outside the brewery.

'Oh, you're not thinking about leaving us, are you?' He sounds genuinely devastated. Elen looks away from his sorrowful, boyish face. He's wearing sweatpants with the insignia of a university rowing team. 'Can I show you something?' Luka holds out a plump, tanned hand to her. She considers taking it and then only laughs and follows him back down towards the boys' room.

It smells of cigarettes and deodorant. It might once have been a meeting room, or a private dining room; it's mostly taken up by a table, onto which Luka hauls something like an old-fashioned doctor's bag. He removes a folded sheet of paper, unfolds it at comical length. It's a map (they're retro, these kids), a map reinforced with panels of cardboard, written over in places, collaged here with newsprint and there with train schedules, and with small squares of scaled-up maps over certain areas. Elen examines these, with what she hopes is due regard for the awed silence being modelled by Luka. Mount Bachelor and the Cascade Lakes Scenic Byway bloom out at her.

'It's a road trip?'

'It's an adventure!' Luka sing-songs, one part mock disappointment, one part true excitement. 'It's ski-squatting mapped out for the rest of the year.' He darts his little finger. 'There's Hintertux, there's Livigno, that was quite resort-y; there's Cerro Castor, there's you! We have a year at least planned. For me, I could do this for ever. I think Lyn could too.'

Elen thinks Lyn could exist spinning through snowpack for a thousand years, and never look old and never crack a smile. 'It's beautiful,' she says. It is, in a demented-scribbling way. 'You've taken quite a strange route. I guess air fare isn't a problem.'

'We follow snow patterns, anti-seasons. So, conflating when the snow's still good with when the mountain's least busy, which can be a tiny overlap. It's not always convenient, or cheap, but we do it for love. And it's actually much more sustainable than resort skiing, not just because Clover donates the price of the flights back to Greenpeace or wherever. Lyn does the maths. She's like a genius with it, or like a man with crazy pins in a map.'

'It's a lovely project,' Elen says, humouring him. It's the voice she uses when she's trying to get a quail out of her nephew's bed. The project is not unlovely, but it jars: she hadn't fully realised exactly how rich these kids were. There have been clues (the clothes, the creams, talk) but only now does she understand that they are, in fact, ski-forever-level rich. Elen reaches for the word – is it Trustafarians who play at being down and outs? Or are they the ones who flit between causes rather than hobbies? These fun new species of zeal are hard to keep up with.

'You could come with us,' Luka is saying. 'You could come the whole way with us; there's room in the car.'

'I'm old enough to be your mother.' She hates herself as she says it. It's a cliché, and not even really true. But Luka won't fall down that conversational pit, he keeps it light and seamless, flutters his long eyelashes at her and says, 'I'm older than I look.'

'You look like a little baby.'

'Oh, I hope not.' He winks. 'I hate prodigies.'

And then his face turns earnest. 'But seriously,' he says. He is sweet, this boy, she does like him. He makes her laugh. He makes her feel at home, in a way none of the others do. 'Everything happens at the right time,' he says. 'I don't believe in any of that woo-woo stuff, but I do believe in that. It means a lot that you're here with us, Elen.'

These kids have the weird habit of inserting her name into their sentences a lot. Perhaps it's a British thing; she's sure she doesn't do that, and neither does anyone she knows. Sometimes it seems a little forced, like they're really holding on to that 'the sweetest sound that anyone can hear is their own name' soundbite. But here it sounds good. Elen doesn't doubt that Luka likes her, and strangely, this fact by itself makes her happy.

She continues to play along. 'Okay, where's next?'

'Canada. Then these gorgeous, gorgeous slopes in Turkey. I think one might be the mountain where Noah crashed his ark.'

She's not even sure if her passport's still valid. 'It sounds wonderful. Obviously, I can't come. You don't need another person on your tour.'

'No, we would love to have you. It's our dream. It's part of the tour, accumulating friends!'

'Converting people to your ski-squatting cause?'

'Exactly. Populating utopia, you know?'

Elen finds the whole incendiary enthusiasm of youth staring at her from out of Luka's face. Menaceless, like a drunk girl in a bathroom saying *Let's be friends for ever.* 'I'll stay for another day, because you're so sweet. But then I'll be off.'

Luka is unperturbed. 'It's good snow tomorrow.'

+++

She's the first to wake. She looks at the ceiling and listens to Clover and Lyn's soft breathing. The room is nearly warm with hours' worth of accumulated body heat from the three of them. She relaxes back into the blankets. The next time she opens her eyes, it's an hour later and they've both disappeared.

Lyn looks up from her coffee when Elen comes down into the canteen. Her pale hair is swept up in a towel. Where has she showered? Elen's almost ready to begrudge her the clean hair (the clear eyes, the perfect nails) but Lyn pushes the Thermos towards her.

'Thanks.'

Clover swings in, dressed in thermals and one of Luka's cheviot pullovers. For one hysterical split-second, Elen deduces that they've been sleeping together. No, it's just that easy rich communalism. Elen is miserly in comparison; she would notice if someone took a pair of her socks – a school friend stole a pair of plastic earrings once, and then lost them on holiday and she still has night angers about it. The idea that someone is getting something and she's getting nothing . . . the idea that she's getting nothing because someone else is getting something: it puts her stomach into seething knots. But it's never an option that George might end up with nothing and so all the teenagers put money into the piggy without looking.

'Oh, are these navel oranges?' Clover asks no one in

particular, sorting through the breakfast stuff Luka has picked up. A small irrational anger threatens to burst out of Elen into the quiet; she smiles to herself instead. I could never live with them, Elen thinks. I'd kill her.

In the sudden wash of slope air – it feels sudden, always – the thought that this may be the last time occurs to Elen. She's familiar with the thought. Over the last two months it has arrested her often: *this may be the last time I set this table; this may be the last time I pull out of this gas station; this may be the last time I can afford to live alone.* But here, following George's slow track up to the high snow, everything blue and green and blindingly bright, it feels newly sad. A little lurch. Luka was right – the snow is good.

Her legs have acclimatised. It's in the ascent that she notices: all at once easier, all at once more pleasurable. I am stronger, Elen thinks. I have quantifiably improved. And then at the top of the mountain she has that feeling like sex, looking down over the first curving pass and letting herself fall.

The addictive, nearly familiar sliding of her stomach as she edges over the tracery George has left. He grins at her, flashing; she's grinning back. Sudden sheerness, then she follows him into the trees, slow bumps over small thick crusts of snow which she thinks must hide the roots. Where's the untracked line? Suddenly a quick perfect steep route through the trees unfolds itself like a language at her; she skirts close to a trunk and then there's pine needles in her teeth, snow in her teeth!

*

In the resort, at their anti-après, the evidence of an under-
lying credo begins to make itself more apparent. Now that
Elen's looking for it she can see little flashes of principle, or
principle-adjacent behaviour. Luka follows a blog on Tor that
tracks squatting news. He lies on his stomach in the corner
of the dining hall and calls out news at it's reported: 'The
Krakelingenweg squat in the Netherlands was evicted. Twelve
arrests.' (Lyn nods, halfway into a shoulder stand. Clover and
George are grating cheese for an experimental stove spaetzle and do not reply.) 'Mozart3 in Freiburg was evicted. No
arrests; demonstrations organised.'

'L'Écharde in Montreuil was evicted. No arrests; demonstrations organised. Now these are not Airbnbs, these are
houses actually going empty, and these are not ski-squatters,
they're very much real squatters,' Luka says to Elen with a
briefly dazzling self-awareness that sets her whole impression
of him off-kilter. 'Although to be fair – at every squat there's
the privileged kid. Like the juggler.'

'A juggler?'

'No, like at every squat there's one privileged kid, like how
at every party there's the guy who juggles. You know, that
guy. Everyone's a bit pissed and all of sudden Ben's reverse
cascading three lemons.' He looks confused at her lack of
comprehension. 'Maybe it's an English thing.'

Elen cackles. Her shins are sore, her eyes shining. She's
been sleeping less than she has in years – that is to say, she's
been awake more hours in the day. Clover had asked her
earlier that day where in town they could buy a spaetzle-
maker and Elen hadn't even wanted to laugh, just made a
guess and sent her on her way. Now with everyone holding

noodles on plastic plates, Clover is tearing parsley off the stem and passing it around: 'Act of love, anybody? Act of love?' And it tastes almost like it.

'Leaving us tomorrow, are you, Elen?' says Luka. He says it the way you would speak to a retiring teacher in assembly, a sort of practised officious regret, but he's smiling.

'I've not been looking forward to the drive, I'll tell you that. And it's been nice skiing again. I was thinking I might stay.'

'Yes!'

'If it's all right with you – just until you leave Bend. Then I'll be on my way.' They can't hear her; they're cheering. She's their beloved mascot grown-up.

George tells her that they are going to organise 'beers' to celebrate. He hands her a glass of wine while they set about organising beers, which seems to not involve any actual beers at all. Limes materialise from an icebox. Someone's sent for sambuca, buried in the snow behind the car (this is gestural, surely – the whole resort's a cold storage system). Lyn and Clover almost really fight over control for the music. Elen shrinks and then unfurls a little; it's all beautiful.

'Wait. What was that?'

The teenagers' laughter subsides. Clover is the last left laughing, a little shriek that flags; Luka closes his eyes as if to better parse the sounds that remain.

'Wuthering?' Clover suggests.

'No. It could be animals maybe. There were a fuckton of birds when we got here, you know.'

'Too heavy for birds.'

'I genuinely can't hear a thing, you guys.'

'It stopped. But it sounded like something falling over. Well, like someone stumbling. Not like. You know. An armoire falling over, or whatever.'

'An armoire, Lyn?'

'It's probably a homeless guy, no? The place is hardly secure. There's barely a front door.'

'All right, listen. It's probably nothing. I'll go check it out; Luka, you stay with the womenfolk.'

'I'll come with you,' says Elen, although a vision of the fifty locked bedrooms unspools before her. Fifty dark cubes.

'No, Elen, please. *Noblesse oblige.*' George bows, like a drunk might blow a kiss, and heads out of the canteen towards the noise in the dark.

'It's definitely nothing,' says Luka. They sit in quiet, all of them, for long minutes. Then the sound comes again – everyone hears it, just a strange jerky sound like boxes being moved.

'What the fuck was that?'

'Now *that* was an armoire falling over.'

'God, Luka.'

Luka looks at Clover biting her lip. 'You know it'll be okay. Nothing bad has ever happened to that boy in his life.' He turns his face, which had been suddenly tender. 'Now, I take my job of tending the womenfolk very seriously, and that is why I'm going to make us some drinks.'

Slightly on edge herself, Elen contemplates making some kind of soothing gesture at Clover but she's been so out of the habit of soothing. And then George walks whistling back in, holding a scaffolding pole.

'Fucking hell, mate. Careful with that thing.'

'I don't think he's going to be bothering us any more.' George twirls the pole like a baton, three foot and iron.

For a moment Elen thinks the black scuff on the end of the pole is blood. He's a big man; it's menacing, how easily he carries it. Without warning Lyn laughs and then everyone laughs, except for Clover, who says, 'So there was no one there?'

'Of course there was no one there, Clovey.'

'You looked all over?'

'I looked all over. I think it might actually have been the wind knocking something over, not to subscribe to Lyn's armoire conspiracy.'

And it's all fine. Elen closes her eyes, laughing. She has no idea who they are at all – George might well have a touch of the Purge about him. But some people run up huge credit card debt when their husbands leave them or sleep with their friends or get bad tattoos, so when she opens her eyes and Luka is standing in front of her with a mixed drink, she takes it. She leans back into the cushion; she drinks.

Chapter 4

It will be a long evening. The last time Elen was at a similar party she'd been dropping her nephew off. That's how it will feel to her by the end, anyway, sitting in circles, playing games, drinks spilt, voices at a frightening pitch, one kid dozing off in the corner (George, full of sambuca). In both cases, some sense that she shouldn't actually be there, though tonight in the resort that sense is allayed by the toast that Luka makes to the extension of her visit.

'To ELEN!'

She has nothing to cheers with; she is topped up.

The kids look even younger when they're not in their ski gear. Luka's shirt appears to be hand-painted; Clover's found the time to slip on a charm bracelet. Perhaps she wears it on the slopes. The games are just the games that Elen knows. It's still strange to see Lyn search for a Never Have I Ever with straight-up teenage vigour. Both reassuring (it's not a psycho cult, they're just kids) and disappointing (they're just kids, they're just kids, they're just kids). 'Never Have I Ever been married,' Lyn says.

There's a little pause to see how this goes down – not much

reference has been made to Robert; in fact, Elen doesn't think they even have his name. But Elen drinks, says something like *Never again*, and Lyn smiles. It's a wonderful co-operation: Lyn has opened a space for Elen to light-heartedly assert her experience, and in so doing has reinforced her own status as the girl who will just go there, etiquette or not. Elen takes a second sip. She's thinking too hard.

'Never Have I Ever ghosted someone,' says Luka.

George drinks to this, and then says to Elen 'Ghosting is basically when you stop—'

'I know what ghosting is. We have the internet over here too.'

He beams. 'Never have I ever jacked off to a mountain.' (Luka raises a bashful glass to his mouth.) 'No no no – never have I ever jacked off to the *thought* of a mountain.' Luka tilts the bottle and swallows.

'Luka's sex mad,' Clover whispers.

It's black like water out. The wind sighs over the snow. Elen's turn. She'll have to do a gentle one, obviously; she doesn't want to sound them out about their coke habits or who's had sex with who. 'Never Have I Ever shoplifted.' There's a long silence.

'Never Have I Ever slept with an older woman,' says Clover. Luka looks unsettled by this one. His emotions translate immaculately. George and Lyn both drink.

Elen feels warm inside. It must be the atmosphere, comradely. The warmth of the student lifestyle she's never had, though they're all a couple years past university. What was she doing when she was this age? Probably much the same thing, but with less expensive alcohol and in the park or someone's parents' house, instead of buried in the mountains of another country.

The whole spell of the haunted resort up in the mountains begins to warp; the fifty abandoned bedrooms are not spooky any more, not really. Instead they give the whole night the feel of an accelerating dream, or of the end of the world. Clover's standing on the table suddenly, in the resort canteen. New game, she says, new game, no more Nevers, and her bracelet's jangling, her beautiful hair is swinging and Luka is looking up at where her thick thermal socks disappear into the kind of long velveteen skirt that the Victorians must have worn at après. God, attractive people really can just wear anything.

'I'd suggest Suck and Blow but I think Elen would change her mind about joining us,' he says.

Lyn appears to Elen in sudden flashes as being somehow more composed than the rest of them but maybe that's just her beautiful stony face. Certainly, she is drinking. Certainly she is drinking mainly ice cold sambuca 7ups poured attentively by Luka who is in charge (self-appointed) of libations and who makes sure each person has their drink with a specialised, individuated care. For Lyn the care reveals itself as partnership: it's co-captainship, it's We're The Only Two Who Really Get It, it's tall in a plastic cup in her cold hand. For Clover it's a special kind of flirting reserved for someone with whom part of the game is the total inconceivability of any actual romantic outcome, and for George, simply that brotherhood that is directed from the smaller and brighter to the handsome and more athletic. For Elen, of course, it's welcome aboard, a sly wink and a shake of the head that acknowledges the adventure isn't as big as all that, it's just a ski holiday, besides which they're on her turf – but still, isn't this all fun? Isn't it wonderful to be one of the gang? And someone's phone is making music in a bowl left behind by skiers years ago, by long-dead hotel staff (certainly not long dead, the resort was only abandoned five years ago – well, no one can really know – anyway, that's how it feels to Clover). The same voice is coming out of each mouth. Elen's next drink is maybe her fourth and she's sinking into that familiar sense of control slippage, the foggy walls sliding up around her as in the kitchen with Robert. Outside, all the mountains are black and the snow is in occasional sashes down the sides of the road and she could tap into that black snowiness, the place that looks down over the place she's from, she could go and have a cigarette, she is on the cusp of a great profound feeling, a foreshadowed nostalgia – but now George and Luka are wrestling with their hands behind their backs, beaming, and throwing shadows up on the resort walls. One is shirtless. And Clover sinks down next to her. 'Elen, I'm so glad you're staying.'

'So am I,' says Elen, and it feels deeply true.

'Even if it's only for as long as we're in Bend.' She sighs. 'Do you know any games, Elen? When we were in France a commis waiter taught us this crazy game. It was called Jacks or Knives or Fives or something.'

'I think my games will all be the same as yours.'

'I don't think so.' She kisses Elen on the cheek and then takes off one fur-collared slipper; she throws it at George. 'George. GEORGE. Cigarette?'

Luka sits down just as Clover skids off to where George

and Lyn are talking to ask him to roll. 'Are you good on the floor down here, Elen?'

She gets the sense that he's checking in. She wonders if Clover was checking in too. Is Elen a liability? She watches Clover throw her arms around Lyn's neck in an almost choke-hold. Clover wasn't checking in.

Elen realises suddenly that she hasn't replied to Luka's question. 'I'm good on the floor. Are you?'

'It's a bit cold. But if you're happy I'm happy. Back in the conference room I keep thinking I can see damp, like, rising off the floorboards.'

'Bit pernickety for a squatter, aren't you?'

'I didn't think Americans had the word pernickety!' says Luka, beaming, thrilled to be teased. 'To be honest, we were talking about maybe seeing about finding some weed? Like, from town?'

'I wouldn't have thought that was up your street. George said you were purists.'

From Luka's face, she wonders if she sounded stern. 'We don't smoke,' he says, 'Like hardly at all. We just thought it would help us sleep, to be honest.'

'There won't be any dispensaries open. What is it, one o'clock?'

Silly boy. He's drunk of course, his eyes are moving wildly in his bright face. He won't have a problem sleeping, he'll pass out in about an hour. And no one's sober enough to drive down to Bend.

'Oh my god. You know, I forget that it's even legal here. That's so fun. But that's not really the good stuff, right?'

She's silent, non-committal. Whoever's in charge of the

music has switched to playing something electronic and it reverbs weirdly off the resort's high ceilings.

Luka persists. 'You don't know anyone who would have, you know, marijuana. Some hash?'

Hash? He's drunk, his eyes are on her, over her shoulder, round the corner. Someone who has hash. Elen thinks of the people that she does know in town, runs through a short list of names. As she counts them, they seem to graduate in how appalled they would be to see her here, now. If Robert's brother . . .

'Sorry, no.'

Luka realises his mistake in pushing, perhaps. He switches back to charm, his eyes suddenly perfectly affixed to her. 'Probably for the best! Just trying my luck with our authentic Bend inhabitant.'

Clover yells something from across the room about how marijuana is a problematic word, designed to keep cannabis associated with Latin America. George, still shirtless from the wrestling, is making a valiant effort to get his sweatpants off before Lyn stops him. 'I don't understand why we're not all totally naked,' he says. 'I mean, Toad Hall, Whistler. Isn't that what we're trying to do here?'

Toad-Hall-Whistler sounds like pure nonsense Englishness but Luka says that George always brings up Toad Hall, Whistler when he's making a move for total nudity, which 'By the way, is not what we're trying to do here. I mean, unless you want.'

Elen tries to smile. The only sense she has is that at any moment this scene could lurch into orgiastic chaos. The energy is high and drunk on itself, the children are drunk on being children abroad. Luka, she imagines, would fuck any one of them; the same is probably true of George, although he might prefer to stick to the girls his age. Clover is smoking, head back, her lower lashes dark and smudged, distinctly spiky. She doesn't look like the young lady of the slopes. She doesn't even look like the young lady who'd broken into a haunted resort complex but then made them all spaetzle. Luka tops Elen up – she hadn't realised the drink was finished. He looks like a wine sprite in the flickering lights of their strange camp. Elen drinks, keeps drinking. Horrible images intrude on her of it happening – the night going west, mouths and tongues and English genitalia everywhere. Everything happens behinds her eyes, like an oil of The Last Judgement. They are all pink atop of one another – spaetzle, gin coming up, lips revealing too many teeth, George's spit all wet in the hollow of Luka's neck . . . She blinks and they are back, safe again, just kids sitting drunk around some lanterns. Is this how your mind warps when you become a divorcée? Or when you hang out with people much younger than you? Elen sees Lyn laugh suddenly, sharply, mouth wide open, and knows why her mind is playing these tricks.

Chapter 5

Elen wakes up feeling a little bleary. Something has shaken her out of a sodden sleep, a finger on her thigh. No, it's the sense of a muscle stretching in the cold. She crawls out of her sleeping bag and leaves the other girls in the room, dead asleep. She'd like to splash some water on her face but she doesn't trust the taps. There are seams of rubbish in the hallways connecting the girls' room to the canteen: plastic bags, takeout containers, stuff that might have drifted there or that might have been left by urbex tourists. An ornate and isolated wall clock on the staircase has been left untouched.

Luka and George are in the canteen, asleep.

'I was looking for coffee,' she tells their prone bodies. She'd rather wake them up than have them be surprised by her or feel intruded upon. They stir in their nest of blankets.

'We failed to make it to our room,' explains Luka, yawning. 'I think we might have gone a little too hard last night. Big mistake.'

George opens one eye and then closes it. He seems to take a second to place her. Then he sits up a little, fumbles for his smoking stuff. 'There's real coffee in the green tote by the stove, Elen. I'd show you but we're too hungover to move.'

'No,' says Luka. 'That's not true.' He struggles into a more vertical position, but finds it unsustainable. 'Okay. Maybe a duvet day for us today. An acclimatisation day. Like on Everest.'

'Do you want?'

'Please god.' They look immediately happier. Elen can feel herself bustling capably, her thermal socks slipping on the floor as she rustles up coffee for the sleepy boys. It's nice, the smell of the coffee in the frozen air. She catches herself feeling collegiate by association.

Lyn comes in dressed for skiing. She looks surprised when Elen wordlessly hands her coffee. 'Don't tell me. They can't move.' The boys make injured noises back at her. 'Clover's complaining of extreme stiffness. It's you and me today.' Her voice reminds Elen of a war telegram in a movie. Elen doesn't rush to change. She imagines that she'd be a weight around Lyn's white neck however quickly she is ready.

'I'll drive if you want.'

'You're not insured,' says Lyn, climbing in front.

'Sorry,' mutters Elen. 'I thought you all were living on the edge.'

Lyn drives well, and as though she hasn't heard Elen. She has an excuse for silent focus, since she's driving on a different side of the road, but Elen is half worried that the silence could turn awkward once they are out of the car, and they have long climbs ahead, just the two of them. It's weird being worried about leaving silences again. For years she's been too old and too tired and too married to have the luxury.

But the ascents occupy them in solidarity, and if their

mouths are open the cold bright glacier air gets in and dries the backs of their throats. Occasionally Lyn does speak, and she decries the unprofessionalism of the boys.

'"Unprofessional"? You're ski bums.'

Lyn laughs. 'Sort of. But Luka has ideals. You've heard his little anti-seasonaire speeches.'

'Sure,' says Elen, gratified by the laugh and short of breath.

'He can talk a great deal about skiing excellence and expansion of the self and bohemianism and the romantic spirit. And dropping off the grid to "pursue distinction in a field you really care about?"' (Up until Lyn trails off into this impression, Elen has thought of their voices as girl rich and boy rich counterparts but she now realises, hilariously, that there is indeed some slight regional variation to their swankiness. She finds herself honestly intrigued by who is city mouse and who is country.) 'But he'll skip a day like this because his tummy hurts. Oh, Clover's worse. She just wants a cuddle.'

Elen assents. She's pleased, sort of, to be included in the halo effect of Lyn's steely professionalism.

It is so still up here. They are off the beaten path but it's more than that. Before the bar, the car, the beer, the *kids*, the last time she'd been up in the Cascades had been on a hike last April with Robert and some of his friends. They'd fallen out of the habit of using the nature around them, Elen scoffing at hiking in particular, but one of his friends had insisted on an intensive, beery 'ramble' for his birthday. And sure, it had been beautiful: birdsong, the juncos twinkling brown in the sky. There'd been snow on the ground but there'd been water too, and the tinkling sound of it running past stones and ice.

Now the snow is still and quiet. Sounds are muffled up this high, and rebound dully off the snowpack. At the top of their track, Elen identifies it as the extensive calm of a prehistoric mountain, or of a padded cell. The trees are mostly bare. In the distance, a corolla of branches has turned wet pink green already. Green not like the jungle, not like not-blue but green like Monet or dollars or like silver or the word frieze. She doesn't realise that Lyn has set off until she's cut in front of her. Elen pushes forwards, skiing towards and past the image of spring.

There's something about following someone down a mountain, the rotation of your hips taking its cue from the rotation of the hips ahead. At the end of the slope there's a fragile closeness between them. And a real exhausted hunger also, the kind that makes babies cry.

'Yes, let's go eat,' Lyn says. 'Where's good?'

'We could ...' Elen points vaguely in the direction of on-piste.

'It's a bad chips and expensive paninis vibe, or ...'

It is. She has a sudden, awful thought that her card will be declined there. When Robert left – having taken nearly everything out of the joint account – she had just under six hundred dollars in her personal, which she's not checked since establishing that she'd be unable to pay rent. Lyn understands that some kind of panic has risen in Elen – her demeanour does not vary but she says, 'Let's go somewhere in town'.

'Somewhere in town?'

'Yes. Luka will be so disappointed in us, anyway, if we do something as seasonaire as go to the ski-café.'

Nothing feels right. 'Be my guest, but I can't join.'

'What do you mean?'

'I'm out, you know, in my head I've left. I'm not running into my brother-in-law at a sandwich shop.'

'Oh.' Lyn considers this. 'Do you have that thing where everyone you see looks like it could be him?'

'I really do.'

'Face-blindness.'

'It's why I'm hiding out with the only people who could not possibly be him. Four British teenagers.'

They eat at Pinnacle Espresso in the end. It's a concrete chunk run through with kids, and the paninis *are* expensive. 'Have you seen pictures of the hotel complex at the top of Snowdon?' ('Pictures of,' is muttered, which Elen takes to be a concession to her Americanness. She shakes her head.) 'Big fuss because one of the royals called it the highest slum in Wales, or something. Pinnacle Espresso is giving it a run though. No, it's okay. Kind of brutalist. Better than a lot of the places we saw in Europe.' When Elen isn't looking Lyn covers the bill wordlessly. They walk back through the snow, in which green things are growing.

The ascents after lunch are slower and more conversational. Lyn is not one of those people who suddenly flowers with warmth and openness once she is asked about herself. Nevertheless, Elen gets glimpses of her life – a cold mother, naturally, and something to do with a mussel boat. She talks more readily about the others; George getting 'miles lost' in Argentina, holding an intervention after Clover admitted that Luka's flirtatiousness made her uncomfortable, where 'anti-seasonaire' had come from. The teenagers, especially Luka, abound with superstitions and principles about skiing, travel, life. '"Passionate People,"' (Lyn quoting Luka), '"always strive towards some useful end such as the increase of wealth or the perfection of work even when they are engaged in leisure activities like skiing."' '"The great goal of the bohemian is expansion of the self."' These kind of Life Philosophies (capital L, capital P) don't bother Elen. Some of it is similar to the hippiness of lots of the people who showed up in Bend; some of it is weirder, more British. Either way, it doesn't scare her. It's kids' stuff. Lyn thinks so too.

The walking is becoming hard work. Elen finds herself thinking that it wouldn't be wrong to let herself fall forward, down into the snow, and lay there for a while. Or, not even that it wouldn't be wrong, but that there would be no consequence, nothing to stop her. She catches the name Fourier for the third time and starts listening properly.

'Basically, Luka was briefly involved with freemasonry at university. I don't think he was massively obsessed by it – just wanted to take some pictures at the, like, masonic lodge and know about all the cloak and dagger stuff that certain tutors who were involved in it knew. In fact, I know he didn't rate it because he was quite anti the whole no-women thing.' Lyn says this last without hiding her tenderness for him.

'But he was still involved. Isn't that quite a process?'

'Oh yeah, all the secret handshakes, blindfolding, learning lines. He had lots of free time. And one of the older gentlemen gave him a book. *The Utopian Vision of Charles Fourier.* It's bright pink and it has "Passionate Attraction" in the subtitle, so he read it. It looked like trash. Like,' – she cast around for the word – 'like pulp fiction, you know. But he loved it. I don't know whether he went and read all the other Charles Fourier tracts that are out there. I doubt it. But, I'm positive – he dropped out of the freemasonry stuff. He spent his time thinking and talking about Fourier. He's slowed it down now and he won't want to scare you off. But I was taking my final exam and I put pen to paper and tried to write and all I could think was *Fourier adored zebras. Fourier believed that children under fifteen should be kept clear of all information on sexual matters. Fourier thought the moon would come to be replaced by five smaller moons.*'

'Oh, so Fourier was crazy.'

'Yes, definitely. But there's other stuff as well. It's about loving what you do. Communal living. Everyone looking out for each other. He had all of these ideas about utopian communities. Of course, it's always the place that gives utopia the trouble. Which is why Luka's so invested in this kind of nomadism. It's not a late gap year, you know.'

They've reached the top of the climb without Elen realising. It sounds like Luka's crazy too (yesterday, his 'populating utopia' comment sounded only whimsical). But before she can remark, Lyn is tearing past her, and this is the last time Elen is going to follow her down the run.

Chapter 6

The cold is the obvious flaw in the dream of it all. The teenagers are in sleeping bags. Elen is awake in the late night or early morning, and the chill runs up her shins. There must be holes all over the resort, she thinks; cracks in windows, whistling walls. Something like a deep breath from the room across the hall: Elen wonders where Clover heard the story about the dead boy, and then decides that it's George, smoking in a half-sleep.

She stretches her aching legs under the blanket. Her husband is in Portland now, is in Olympia, is in Victoria, Canada. He is washing the dishes in another woman's sink or putting Splenda in a foreign coffee cup. He is asleep. His glasses flash on a million desks. They are in Portland, or they are back in the red cabinet of the house in South Bend, or they are in the skip under snow. The cold cream is lying easy on Lyn's neck.

+++

Elen finds herself alone at the top of the slope, almost without realising. She looks down at the mountain disappearing in front of her. The descent, she knows, will be over in minutes.

She will climb it again. On the ascent, the ice underneath the snow makes it blue and creaky. She will climb it again.

Two, three junco sparrows take off across the sky from somewhere east. The darkness is warm, the shrewdness dissipating; Elen lifts one ski, then the other, sets them softly down again on a mountain that she knows and will learn. The snow keeps the mark of them.

Chapter 7

François Marie Charles Fourier (called Fourier by most people, and Marie by George) did claim that the moon would come to be replaced by five smaller moons. He also originated a specific utopia, and had practical designs to put it into place. In Fourier's vision, people co-operated and were happy. They lived together in large phalansteries, or 'grand hotels'; the people doing the hardest jobs lived on the top floor and the people doing the easiest jobs on the ground floor and people's jobs were chosen according to their passion. Passional living was Fourier's chief dream. As he understood it, the only solid ground on which to base a moral position was the principal of pleasure. All creative activity, including industry, craft, agriculture, would arise from liberated passion.

At first, the citizens of these utopias would have friendly relations with the outside world, on nodding terms or an informational tourism basis. The end goal, however, was iron curtains about the place, although it was the place that gave Fourier the trouble. That's usually the case with utopias. Hence, apparently, the cartoonishly expansible map – Hintertux, Oregon, Alberta, Turkey. For Calvino, an admirer of Fourier, utopia isn't solid enough to be found. It must be looked for, hanging shadowy, suspended, crepuscular in the corner of ideas, 'a utopia of fine dust'.

('Hello?' Luka'd said, his chest warm on Elen's shoulder as he stirred sambuca into her drinking chocolate. 'A utopia of fine dust? Powder. He's talking about off-piste.'

'Luka's not joking, Elen, he's just batshit,' Clover had said.)

But Fourier's blueprint had practical ambitions. He was pragmatic enough to pronounce that 'to object to the throne or the altar is useless and damaging', and to encourage a distribution of one third of all profits to capital investors. Work was to be adored. The reason work was naturally hated was because from morning to night five days a week, workers were in the same grim, cramped space. If work could be transitory, it would be different. And so: Livigno, Cerro Castor, Bend.

'Forgive me,' Elen had said. (She'd been in the resort with the teenagers for two weeks now and had picked up two verbal tics: interrupting people with an ironic 'forgive me,' and finishing a sentence with 'no?' But this last sounded so affected that she would break off as soon as she realised she was saying it and make an adult American half cough. It wasn't her fault, Clover had said, and put a hand round her waist. 'It's very intense, two weeks and just five people. Have you had that thing yet where all your dreams are just about us?' Elen shook her head in a way that suggested the undoing of two weeks of companionship.) 'Forgive me, but what work are you doing, exactly?'

'Well, that comes later. We're doing the passion bit now.' Of course. If Elen sounds out their creed at any length she starts feeling shrewd and then she feels old and then poor, so she tends to minimise her interruptions.

'And the community bit,' Clover adds. 'A phalanx needs more than five members to be sustainable, on the work front.'

Luka is clearly the main adherent, although Clover does genuinely adore the communal living aspect. She hates an empty flat, pities the isolated family. When Luka talks about the phalanstery, she gets quite excited, truly believing that they will all live together and raise their children together. 'Harmonism,' Fourier calls it, and 'Harmony Chamonix,' says George. The children will benefit from the intersection of all their knowledges and be skiing, French-speaking, Fourier-spouting virtuosos ... George will tell them Greek and Roman myths to get them to bed. Ah, Elen thinks. Rich crossbred genius baby. She imagines Clover's kid, beautiful hair, dark eyes, talking Latin at four like a little Tudor prince in a snowsuit. Born out of touch. She imagines him tumbling off the side of a mountain.

Fourier classified sexual manias and gastronomic interests. He'd been obsessed with classification, sorting every societal intrigue into genus and type. There were thirty-odd kinds of cuckolded man, for example, and seventy-two kinds of financial ruin. If Elen were to have the inclination, there would surely be some Fourierian almanac that she could consult on her dreams. Of course they've all been about the teenagers. Good catch, Clover. As for the genus? Broadly: 1. *anxiety dreams* (they have left without telling her; she has the wrong equipment; the resort canteen is full of spiders; her teeth are falling out), 2. *nightmares* (the resort canteen is full of shadows; Robert is bleeding, pulling the blankets off her), 3. *skiing dreams* (all similar, the snow won't stop coming towards her and different birds get in her way, she is woken sometimes by her hips moving in time with the turns of the dreamed route, 4. *Lyn* (Lyn; Lyn; sometimes intersecting with category one or three). The dreams she's had in the resort outnumber the nights she's spent there. It's the altitude and the mountain air. A fact well known in Bend: skiers and expeditioners report vivid, unusual dreams at a staggering frequency.

Curiously, despite conceding Fourier's reputation as the original utopian socialist, the teenagers would never otherwise say the words communist or socialist. They would never decry the systems they believe to have made Britain great or their parents rich. In college Luka slept in a Che Guevara T-shirt, but George plays with stocks. But when the kids work like a well-oiled machine, as they occasionally do – Clover on washing up and George with the kitchen towel, Lyn moving a black brush over the floor; two hopping out of the Prius with bags of food and two more replacing them to carry the bottles of milk and the wine out of the car boot – Elen laughs because she's watching them do everything that any normal kids who live alone should do, albeit with a little more vigour, a little more joy, but she knows that Luka's watching them and thinking: we're a phalanstery! We're a smooth-running commune, a Fourierian production line with a mop and a bucket of dish soap!

It is different though, for Elen. There was something about waking up and not immediately thinking about all the mess she has to clear up alone. The thing about washing up is that it's the whole human condition. The thing about washing up is it's never done. Robert would go to the bank. He would leave his empty bowl lashed with milk on the table, a little reproach. Sorry about your sad breakfast before you go gallivanting into the daytime, Elen was forced to think, five days a week. She'd been in the habit of making breakfast once upon a time, or putting toast on the table. But this was that much more dishwashing to do. She was a homemaker – she had been. But she had always been missing some of the requisite parts. She assumed that was why Robert had never pushed the idea of children. The thought of the dishes sat on her shoulders very blackly. The house was devoid of light. It could be such a nice house to spend time in – the mountains like a postcard outside – except that when it was full of trash, it was full of trash. She'd been able to waste three hours thinking about dishes that needed twenty minutes to do. And towards the end she would sometimes think, Okay, I'll have a little pop of medicine. And she would pour herself a drink – two drinks, one to enjoy by itself, and one to sip while she worked – intending to play a nice song and make a thing of the tidying. But then after the dishes there were the surfaces. Now, the thing with surfaces is they're the whole human condition.

Still, Elen can make tea the way that Luka likes it, and it doesn't feel like service, it feels like an act of friendship. Or something on the way to being friendship. There are things about herself that she will never teach them; there are things about them that she will never respect. But two weeks has made a great deal of difference. She knows which of George's coughs are real and which are for comic effect; she no longer shocks each time Clover lets down her beautiful hair. When it comes to Lyn, the part of Elen that is hyperactively observant quiets down. But she has come to an approximate knowledge of Lyn these past weeks, which is to say that she knows the feelings of Lyn inside her, fingers down throat.

(A lazy afternoon after the weather turned bad early. Three jigsaws with forty missing pieces thrifted from some junk store. Lyn demonstrating how to use a tongue scraper, cleaning it off with her fingers. The scraper was a weird contraption, looking basically like a cross between a wishbone and a potato peeler. It was made, naturally, of pure copper. Elen had been living with the kids long enough to know that pure copper was balancing as well as antimicrobial.

'This seems like it would be more up Clover's street than yours,' she'd said.

'What do you mean?'

'Whatever you call it, homeopathic medicine. Hippie dippy.'

'Hippie dippy, oh my god, Elen. "You're such a card", is what I'd say, if I could speak your language.' A rare Lyn smile as her hands had worked the soft blade of the tongue scraper.

'But you know what I mean.' It's what she'd thought of the smooth stone Lyn used to knead the knots out of her muscles.

'I suppose. This is science though, not just good vibes. While you sleep your impurities rise out through your tongue. That's why it's all furry when you wake up.' (Elen had winced). 'It works best when you have a hangover. You know how a tongue gets after a hangover. Just poisonous. Look – open up.'

She'd opened her mouth, suddenly conscious of a recent cup of wine. Lyn had reached inside and positioned the scraper at the back of Elen's throat. There was a moment of nearly giggly shared consciousness. It had been like two girls touching tongues, not kissing, at a sleepover. Wine in her teeth, Lyn's fingers on her mouth. She hadn't been touching her insides, exactly; there was no finger-to-tongue contact, only the cold bronzey taste of the scraper ... but her thumb had been under Elen's chin, tilting her mouth up and open. It was over pretty quickly – two drags over the tongue, and then Lyn had flipped the scraper in a business-like manner to show Elen the little white silt of plaque that had come off her tongue. Before it had ended, the moment had transformed. It had seemed like it would fit in a certain series of imagined applications: Lyn sweeping her rose-quartz face roller over Elen's cheekbones, cold on skin sending a feeling straight to her gut; pressing the jade stone into the sore arches of her feet; running copper over her tongue. All eroticised moments of care. But it occurred to Elen that in practice it felt like nothing so much as letting Lee paint her face or plait her hair.)

It's like she's caught in Lyn's orbit, more than anything else. A pleasant inaction; a stalemate. Elen is content to circle her from a fixed distance, abob in outer space.

It hadn't been like this before. As a teenager at school, a real teenager, Elen had felt girl-crazy in the clunkiest, most internal way. It pooled on the floors of her body and felt cold and slimy inside of her – not from shame, but from the sheer extent of her wanting. Every breast on the street drew her helpless eye. She copied them into notebooks from the pages of dirty magazines. (She was not an artist.) She tried to get off to her own body, which was the body of a girl. In practice, this looked like putting duct tape over most of the mirror so that she could

only see a stomach, a floating nipple. This was awful. Elen
watched her boy friends start to date, or to fool around. When
she hung out with them after school they were orbited by new
familiar faces. Elen watched them eat chips out of the packet
and slip those same greasy hands under the back of a camisole,
or paw too hard at the inner seam of a jean when they thought
no one was looking, and she thought: I would treat you better.
I'm cleaner, better-smelling. My hands are softer.

One of her guy friends took pity on her and that was all
it took. They'd all gone to Lansing for the night and he had
pulled strings. It was weeks in the making, he told Elen;
minimum three conversations with a friend of a friend of
somebody who knew an apparent lesbian. She was very
grateful, she told him, and smacked the cap off his head even
though she was telling the truth. It never bothered Elen that
the first girl she loved also happened to be the first lesbian
she met. Their compatibility was not a questionable thing.

Liberty was chiefly sweet. She was a pretty blonde girl,
the year above Elen, about to start at a teacher training
college. She was a swimmer. When Elen thinks of her, it's
always of her long bright hair, slightly stiff at the ends from
chlorine. Liberty was a real femme, a girl with girl friends
who all regarded Elen the way they would regard a straight
boy. Sometimes she felt that was how Liberty regarded her
too. (She wonders at the difference between her presentation
then and her presentation now. What does Lyn see? Was it
marriage that had changed her, or time and age? Certainly
she feels more womanly these days, even if only a little, or
only indefinably; or at least more reconciled with the fact
of her womanhood.) If Liberty viewed Elen as masculine, it

translated into a slight neediness, the way a girl can be anxious when a boy is withholding. Liberty was 'cute', and totally aware of the effect she had on boys, with her waist-length, crispy hair, but miraculously focused on Elen. She instructed her sexually in a low voice with the curtains drawn. These were moments that Elen would return to for fifteen years.

There were issues, obviously. They lived too far apart and both with their parents, which made the whole thing exciting and difficult. They never said the word 'girlfriend'. Elen would sit fuming with desire in her bedroom, bristling every time she heard her mother move downstairs. Thump – her mother would close the fridge door, and it was like a stabbing pain to her. Elen and Liberty slept at friends' houses, on rooftops. Once in the basement gym of an apartment building. Some school friend of Liberty's, who had an apartment in Lansing in a fancy block with concierges and a computer room, had promised that they could take the bed; but she was nowhere to be seen once they arrived. Liberty took Elen by the hand and led her past the front desk to the unlocked gym, a tiny room that would remain with Elen always. Mirrored walls – five treadmills and a rowing machine – the smell of sweat and plastic. They scrunched up together in the dark on the fun-size couch, getting each other off until they were able to fall asleep. When they were woken up (by bright lights and a sympathetic woman who nevertheless would not forgo her pre-office workout), they had deep imprints on their skin: couch seams and thumbprints.

It was a good first love. Wild crazy highs, disproportionate to their stimuli. Elen remembers the year with Liberty most of all as the feeling of being young and invulnerable. They danced every weekend. They spent their nights in Lansing, which was liberal enough, though they were hardly holding hands. Liberty took her to the zoo once and Elen felt like she was pretending to be on a normal date, but when they were dancing they were perfect.

The issue was mainly distance, although it didn't help during the last few months that Liberty was working hard and Elen was not. There was also the fact, though Elen wouldn't admit it, that she couldn't picture a future with a woman. Not that she was opposed – but that she didn't know what it could look like, and struggled to imagine. Maybe she'd just been lazy. Of course, when they broke up Elen was devastated. She thought she'd never get over it; she had a light spell of heavy drinking and slept around a lot. Meeting Robert a few months later had been totally, overwhelmingly calming. Except for the slight flaring anxieties every time she was in public with him that she would bump into Liberty. It was the same kind of fear that had turned her face-blind in Bend after Robert had left, thinking from a distance that every middle-aged man was his brother. She slowed up behind blonde girls and crossed the street. She knew what Liberty would think if she saw Elen with a man: that she was an itch that had been scratched. This wasn't the case, of course; though it was true that Elen no longer felt like a deer in headlights at every gape in the blouse of a woman leaning forward. Until Lyn, but. Theirs is a stalemate.

(Obviously, Elen is not stupid. Obviously, as much as Elen knows George's coughs or Clover's locks or the weight of

Lyn's fingertips at her lips, she also knows that every thrill of connection is probably simply a superficial response to being suddenly single. Or separated; abandoned, whatever. Alone. But she doesn't mind playing along. She could join the little band of brigands and spend forever like this. Lyn would bathe her eyes with camomile tea to soothe snow-blindness.)

Chapter 8

Some nights, sleeping in the girls' dormitory puts Elen on edge. She knows that her breath is mingling with theirs in the corners of the room; she's unwillingly aware of proximities as soon as the door closes on the three of them. One morning she zones out, looking at the back of Lyn's head as Lyn applies sunscreen, and when they meet eyes in the mirror Elen feels oddly like she's been caught. The last time she'd slept next to another woman's body, it had been Liberty's. She catches herself doing strange things to signal that she's not watching the girls change, pretending to look out the window, or paying sudden attention to the debris under her nails. All this, even when she knows they don't care, even when Clover offers to help wash her hair with stove-boiled water over the sink. (The showers of the haunted resort are, naturally, out of order.)

In the liquid stretches before she wakes up, when all her thoughts are too elastic to be assigned a moral value, she thinks that it's just neat, waking up alone with women. That extra part of your brain that's in operation when a boy's in the room is still asleep. Not that Elen's exactly wary of the boys across the hall. But there's suddenly so much more at play when they're in the mix, so much more to be observed: watching how close the girls and boys get to each other; watching their circuits, their casual touches, their barbs; watching one sip from another's mug, one put a hand in another's pocket. Sometimes it strikes her as madness. They're young, and close in every way – they live on top of each other. Surely at least two of them are hooking up!

Perhaps this is her own generational hang up. Stupid. Hypocritical, even, given that when Elen was in the habit of having friends they were always boys, and that the closest she's felt to another girl was when they were having sex. When Clover combs her fingers through George's hair, it's not because she's a girl and he's a boy. She'd do it for Elen, with shampoo and hot water, if Elen would only let her.

+++

Like drinking, and certainly in combination with drinking, there's a kind of love that can make you come apart. So much of your thinking hangs on someone else: on something of your body, outside of your control. You're constantly trying to stay abreast of another person's interiority. This kind of love, the insecure kind, is usually love in its first or last stages: waxing love or waning love. This hadn't much been the case with Liberty but, towards the end of her marriage (before she cut out caring) Elen had found herself coming apart in such a way. It was like chasing smoke, she'd thought, if that smoke gave you ciphered clues, made eyes, rolled over towards you in the middle of a sleep that could have been deep and could have been fake.

When she'd first felt herself coming apart during these months, Elen papered over the frayed parts with beer and vodka and sleeping in. It would be very easy to go crazy, she'd thought. She'd started speaking to herself when Robert was at work and it came very naturally, beginning with just a *potatoes, potatoes, potatoes* when she started on dinner and growing to a plaintive refrain of *love me* that she hadn't noticed until a cashier was saying 'Excuse me ma'am?' It hadn't bothered Elen that she might be going crazy, only that this unhappy, irresolvable coldness had suddenly stolen into their house. Thinking everything over on the toilet, she wrote *Don't Nag* on the top of her thighs as a reminder to herself. Robert would never see it there, she thought (or said), and then she was angry again and they were both horrible in the evening. She missed him at work and hated him at home.

One day, when there were no guests in the little shed, Elen let herself in and lay down on the strange, uncomfortable bed. Robert's image appeared to her. She watched him lay over her, settle down between her legs, press his head into her thin chest. She cradled his head closely. Though of course he wasn't there, she moved her hands as though he was, over the phantom head. She could feel his warm ears. 'I love you, I love you,' she said to the empty room. That incident worried Elen a bit, and not just because it had pitted her whole stomach out from her with sadness. Talking to yourself was one thing but this time she'd really felt that he was there. She cut out vodka in the afternoon, largely put an end to losing time and (largely) kept in touch with reality; there were only a handful more of those sort of fantastical instances thereafter. Houseflies multiplied on unwashed dishes, washed dishes became unclean of their own accord, someone seemed to be moving in the vacant guesthouse. As long as Elen knew these things weren't real, she wasn't crazy just for seeing them. At night she could hear her mother talking; not to Elen, just talking, and as though in another room. That had been embarrassing but not unbearable. The only unbearable thing was the despair, which was sane and reasonable: the understanding of the end of love. Feeling it leak unstoppably away from both of them, like money. She'd been fully and rationally overpowered by the hot dark load of how sad she was while babysitting Lee one afternoon. God, she'd bribed him half-heartedly with a Twizzler not to tell his mom about her bawling. Maybe it had even worked. In any case, that feeling of waning love had been suddenly muted shortly afterwards and the last year or so was easier to bear and devoid of visions or voices.

When, at last, Robert had left (vanished in the night!), the sense that she was beginning to lose it returned. It was different this time: not hallucinations, just a thread that had come loose somewhere and thoughts that leapt from violence to blankness in seconds. And this time Elen wasn't even a bit worried. In moments of vodka-soda clarity she could observe her train of thought falling apart almost as though from outside of her body. It was like it was happening to another person. She observed her body like it was another person's too. It was unfamiliar to her; it had aged without her noticing. There were new spots and all her hairs had sharper ends.

When your body isn't your own, it's so easy to submit to hot and jumping thoughts. Why shouldn't you do whatever your dazed head tells you? When a body isn't real you feed it wrong, water it wrong, send it off with strangers. She was

a ghost filled with beer and chips and hot dogs and under-
cooked pasta. Funny, honestly, that the strangers to whom
she'd negligently assigned care of herself during her last little
lurch of craziness, the holdover from a long-waned love, were
beginning to make her feel real again.

+++

The other repercussion of treating your body like it's not
your own is that it begins to smell. Elen's been showering
sporadically using baby wipes and Lyn's dry shampoo and
stand-up washes over a pot of boiled water, but the small
rotation of clothes she's brought are beginning to stink at the
pits. Luka tells her they use a laundromat in town. They must
have actually crept out to use it; she plays with the idea of
teasing him – his betrayed commitment to the closed circuit
of the phalanstery! – but he looks embarrassed already. She
knows she will not go to the laundromat; every part of her
body remains resistant to the idea of going into central Bend.
Not only has she skipped town by now in her own mind, but
she's been gone long enough that anyone she ran into would
ask where she's been. To see Robert's brother, to see any one
of Susannah's friends ... impossible. Something about the
actual smell of her worn clothes stops her from immediately
asking whoever next goes into town to put on a washing load
for her. The accumulated odour is shameful, almost pubes-
cent: too intimate to put in the hands of these kids whose
sunscreens are scented. But the problem of the dirty laundry
begins to intrude on her and on the dreamlike cycle of life at
the resort (her mother could be doing her laundry right now).
She asks Luka for the favour after a day of skiing where the

smell of herself had come over her again, warm and close as she'd skimmed through the snow.

Handing the small bag of clothes over feels like giving soiled dressings to a nurse. The thermals she's just peeled off are still warm. Again, she thinks – how little she balks at now. Her body's not her own and its clothes are not her own and nothing is at risk. That said, Luka is at Cascade Cleaners for quite a while, with what amounts to (she calculates) nearly half the belongings she has with her. She's in the canteen with George when he gets back and tries not to act like she's been waiting.

'You've been ages,' says George, helpfully.

'I ran into those Californians. These influencers that we met at some restaurant. Before your time, Elen. The girl with pink hair's missed her period, by the way. She thinks she might be carrying Georgie Junior.'

'Shut up.'

'She wasn't there actually. She's downtown, doing some wholesome bike tour. The guys I saw today were taping passers-by, interviewing them about local superstitions.'

'I didn't know we had local superstitions.'

'Not that local. I think they're going to film some creepypasta thing at Crater Lake. People going missing, cursed flotsam, so on.'

'I love that shit,' George says, wilfully oblivious to Luka's tone.

'I hate those people. It's always some con.'

'You seem like you'd be quite into a video cycling tour of downtown,' says Elen, not sure that influencers are very different from Luka, or from any of the other tourists who show up in Bend, zealous about nature or wellness or something.

'They're swindlers. It's misdirection: oh, how entertaining is this, give me money; hi, look at my smile, I care about you, buy this toothpaste.'

'It sounds more like you hate magicians,' says George.

Luka fixes him with such a sinister stare that the gloom of the canteen seems to intensify. Then he turns to Elen. 'Do you want to see a magic trick?'

She nods obediently. She couldn't laugh if she wanted to: Luka-as-magician draws quiet up around him, a weighty pall of it. He produces a quarter from his pocket, holds it in one tan hand – the porcelain trembles on the shelves – and makes it disappear.

It's very impressive for what it is. It's not any of the coin disappearing tricks that Elen knows, not up his sleeve or in his other hand. If she thinks about it, she can't guess how he's done it at all.

'That's not swindling,' she points out, as he starts to leave. 'You told us you were going to do a trick and then you tricked us.'

'Wrong. It was a swindle to which you agreed.'

'Okay, that was a good vanishing,' says George. 'But now you have to bring it back.'

But Luka disappears down one of the long dark corridors, leaving Elen with a warm bag of her clean clothes.

That night, he insists that the teenagers show Elen their collection. He has by far the most, he fans them out like dollar bills. Clover's stack looks paltry in comparison, which surprises Elen; at the end of the day, she seems like a girl who would like a pretty picture. But Clover's deficit is explained by the fact that she's the only one who ever sends her postcards.

'Postcards are like angels,' Clover says. 'Messages from another world.'

'Formalistically demanding,' says Luka.

'Always getting stuck to fridges,' says George.

'It's a shame you never send any.'

'Lyn, you should send one to your mum,' Clover says, and Lyn stares at her.

'I think she'd have a heart attack.'

'Lyn doesn't even text her mum,' Clover explains. 'She doesn't know if Lyn's in Oregon or the Sahara. Or dying in a crack den somewhere. It's actually very sad.'

'I think she knows Lyn would never touch crack,' says Luka. Clover looks unhappy but she lets it drop. He turns a postcard over in his hands, a photo of the Thermalbad Hintertux with baths the size of stamps, and says, 'They're just too nice to send.'

Poor mothers, thinks Elen. Even this fragment of their vacation they can't bear to part with; they must keep for themselves. Watching Luka heft the postcards appreciatively puts her in mind of the passion she felt towards the old plastic earrings after her friend had lost them.

Luka's whimsy reveals new contours constantly. By now Elen knows which bits of the Fourier narrative don't interest her (Dostoyevsky was nearly executed for his part in planning a Fourierian utopia with the Petrashevsky Circle, and Elen doesn't care at all), and which bits she likes to sit down for, with a tall drink. It seems to her that Luka had been able to use

Fourier to genuinely identify a lot of the things wrong with the world, and had then used these to deduce that the solution was an endless, parentally funded ski holiday. To her knowledge, he's never touched on the idea that the 'passion' with which he wants to resist these Wrong Things (a carousel which rotates but usually involves inequality) might radiate privilege. Elen suppresses her sense that a piece is missing. She believes Luka's Brighter Future chat; she doesn't lose sleep wondering what's behind it, what it is that could drive someone who's so obviously got everything he's ever wanted. The more she can't figure out why a boy like that needs a new world, the more she feels like she's being drawn into something that can't last. The more she likes the kids, the more she feels the draw. It's becoming increasingly difficult to hold on to being shrewd and separate.

The other teenagers play along with Luka. Sometimes it's hard to gauge what's authentic interest and what's humouring him. Sometimes it's not.

'He literally coined the word feminism,' Luka would say. 'And he was hugely sympathetic to lesbians, for his time.'

'He died on a cross for our sins,' Lyn would say back.

'He was massively antisemitic,' George would add, in the same lilting, reverent tone.

Whenever this is brought up, Luka insists that the antisemitism is one of the many bluffs that Fourier wrote in, to turn his text from a straightforward book into a kind of codex. Scholars have theorised that Fourier's works are intentionally difficult to understand: bastard, composite writings made up of mathematics, jokes, facts, histories, lies, wishes. His first book, *The Theory of the Four Movements*, was considered by everybody (and retroactively labelled by Fourier) a riddle. The next books combined early socialist theory with predictions of strange astrological happenings

'You're sounding VQ, mate.'

'VQ?'

'Very Q,' George says.

'Sorry, Luka,' Lyn says. 'I don't think anti-Jewish rhetoric is as obviously ridiculous to a nineteenth-century French guy as the idea of five moons.'

'No, I'm sorry. I didn't realise you were an expert on nineteenth-century France.'

'He advocated for a return to Palestine,' says George.

'Literally with the Rothschilds!'

Luka is getting sincerely upset. His voice is higher than usual. George, Elen has realised, knows the shape of every one of Luka's shortcomings. He is fond of them, he coaxes them to the surface, and then dismisses them with a great roaring slap on the back. He winds Luka up, lovingly and by means she has not yet fully understood.

(One evening, for example, George unveils five fruit popsicles purchased in town and hidden in the freezer until pudding. The big reveal is partly due to the similarity between these specific ice lollies and the Calippos of Old England, unavailable in the States and yearned for by the kids. Lollies are lollies, thinks Elen. Identical, and an infantilising word to say aloud. (The teenagers are guilty of a sneaking kind of nationalism. It hides itself very subtly in their whole ski-creed. They're rebelling against a perceived American modernity, Instagram and destination holidays. The old English secret is not the hedge witch.) But she nabs a blue raspberry ice and watches George attack Luka from the back.

'I got your favourite!' he says. In a weirdly erotic moment, Luka closes his bright eyes and lets George, one hand almost paternalistically on his shoulder, push the rod of coloured ice out of its cardboard tube and into his mouth. 'Can you tell?'

Luka keeps his eyes shut while he slurps. All of a sudden his face freezes.

'Watermelon!' says George, ecstatically. Luka opens his eyes, takes the lolly out of his mouth. He doesn't say anything for the rest of the night, but he's truly angry. The whole incident is too odd to mention. Elen puts it down to a delayed homophobic response.)

In most of these instances, by the time George has laughed and moved affably on, Luka will have a couple more hours of continuing to fume. But then he too will have to stop thinking on it; there are preparations to be made.

Their time in Oregon is coming to an end. It's a fifteen-hour drive to the Rockies. They throw around notes about what to expect – 'complex snowpack', 'prone to avalanching' – and Elen begins to understand that she is coming with them. Mountains have histories, Luka says again and again. Things are preserved up there, old geologies and perfect bodies. After Bend they're headed to Banff, a town in Alberta which is paired with a crater on the moon. They talk about the moon before they go to sleep. They talk about the mountains on the moon, the lunar Alps and lunar Apennines, Mons Huygens. They talk about skiing on mountains on the moon, with a Musk-like zealotry that lasts ten minutes every evening. It's with no more excitement than they once talked about Bend; they're just moving on to the next toy.

But Alberta is the phase between Bend and the moon. Banff and Canmore were the two choices originally, both minutely populated towns twenty minutes from each other by car. Elen listens to the teenagers mathematically divine which is the better option.

'Look, there were 20,000 people at university and it felt like every face was familiar. There are 7000 people in Banff. Canmore's only a little bigger. If we show up people are going to want to know where we're staying.' 'That's crazy talk, George. They're mountain towns. People are in and out all the time. And not every face at uni was familiar.'

They gather in the girls' room for its weak warmth. When Luka leaves for the bathroom, George seizes his madly annotated map. He goes through it, nodding smartly. 'Lake Minnewanka, hoho. Lake Minnewanker.' Clover frowns, but he continues, until Elen asks what the Columbia Arsefield is. The Columbia Icefield, it transpires, is a glacial mass in the Rocky Mountains. Miles and miles of layers and layers of ice, lying partly in the tip of Banff's National Park; formed into perfect ramps almost 150,000 years ago.

'That's some old ice,' says Clover.

'That sounds very up your street. Why isn't it on Luka's agenda?'

'Ah. It's very tough, mostly. I mean, you have to be really good at skiing.'

'You guys are really good at skiing,' says Elen, wondering if they're making the concession to appeal to her.

'No,' says Lyn, with real emphasis. 'We're not really good. We're passionate; we're disciplined sometimes, but really good is rare.' She crosses her legs. 'We've not ever trained. Well – Vince – Luka's brother was at ESF I think. Second *étoile*.'

'*Deuxième*,' says George waggishly.

'*Excusième?*' says Luka, who at that point walks back into the girls' room. The laughter is followed by a silence that Elen can't place. A still panic.

The subject is soon changed back to the moon: George says he hopes Charles Marie is right and there are five of them, and Clover tells them that lunar skiing could be all that's left, that the Earth will probably be uninhabited in a generation and a half.

'Do you think so?' says Elen.

George turns round to explain that Clover's 'very climate anxious, the angel. She was reading – what was it – "Future Options for Snow Production in Tyrolean Ski Resorts" on the plane here.'

It's a younger person's anxiety, Elen supposes; the twenty odd years she has on them have trained her out of guessing about the future. 'How do you deal with that?' she asks anyway. 'Thinking the Earth's going to be empty?'

'Easy,' says Lyn. 'You either learn as many languages and have as much sex as you can, or you just commit politically and kill yourself. Well. George probably thinks he'll be invited to Space Colony B, New New England or whatever.'

'I might be.'

'But Clover has hope.'

In the end, they settle on a bolt of newbuilds scattered in the foothills between the two towns. These are mostly vacation rentals, so they reason that new faces won't disturb anyone.

Two of the houses are a little more remote. Clover begs them to pick Groleau – 'It means Big Water. It feels right.' – but Groleau has a little jacuzzi, which means maintenance, which means a pool guy. They plan on first trying the other house, Hanneke ('Who is naming these chalets?'); if that doesn't work, they'll hit up the rest of the newbuilds until they find one that does. There's no big reveal of Elen's coming, no toast. It's just made obvious at some point. Luka's little assertions ('and we'll put the stove on George's lap if Elen takes the middle seat') graduate in certainty.

In the same way, when they do leave Bend, it's no big moment. It's only a series of practical arrangements (clearing out the dormitories, shaking down the haunted resort for any spare equipment that might come handy), and the anticipation of change solidifying into a reality. Loading the boot, getting in the car – everything Elen does feels both natural and inevitable.

They drive out early past Hawthorne station, which recalls to her every journey out of Bend taken in the last fifteen years. She can count them on ten fingers, it seems.

'Goodbye, house,' calls Clover.

Goodbye. Elen will miss her nephew and his bed of quails and no one else.

Chapter 9

+++

Clover had left behind a small flat in Vauxhall that felt windowless. It was a point of pride for her parents that she didn't need to rent out the second bedroom and so she spent the evenings with no one to talk to, accosted all the time by bad news which she couldn't stop reading. She knew rationally that the news had always been this bad and that it just now happened to be accessible on all channels and 24/7, but it seemed very much that the world was in a state of collapse. Seeing the red on the outlet switches drove her into guilty panic and, there being no one in her flat to counteract her, she spent a lot of time in the dark with all the heating off. She was inclined to minimalism but then didn't understand why her room looked so empty. She worked for a serious cyber-defence firm. It had been exciting for a month, but before she knew it her circuits had reduced to a very few streets; her routine to five or six threads. The loneliness that she felt wasn't the disenfranchisement she'd rationally imagined, reading about big cities as a child in Kent – glamorous loneliness, signs flashing through wet nights, psychics and bodegas, every other door a party. It was Brexit talk and tearing up in Sainsbury's.

She would spend the week looking forward to the dinners and parties but at a certain moment in the evening everyone would invariably begin trooping to the bathroom in twos and threes and she would leave soon afterwards. Cocaine made her very sad. Her no-spend year was a direct recourse to sensing all this excess, this sickness, but that was very depressing too, in its own way. She cycled everywhere in the same silk-blend palazzo pants which wore very thin and which she could not then replace. (Of course, her parents sent her some things she really needed, new towels and her oil paints from home.) No one else seemed happy. Her firm had been recently targeted by several claims of having created a hostile work environment, with billions of pounds now at stake; she didn't know all the details, but it seemed to weigh a lot on everyone. The COO had run out on his wedding, presumably from stress.

More than anything, Clover wanted to be very good at her job. She read *Atomic Habits* and atomised her habits accordingly. Everyone in her world was obsessed with productivity. The Hobonichi Techno was the most coveted planner in her office. It was an obscenely expensive notebook with inspirational quotes in Japanese and invisible lines separating your twenty-four-hour To-Do list from your twelve-hour To-Do list from the horizontal box where you bullet journaled your thoughts and dreams. Clover bought it without thinking and drew little clowns in the margins with Elizabethan ruffs that took up half a page.

Casual sex didn't appeal to her and as a result she was barely touched at all that first year in London. But she loved other girls; any girls who helped her kill the time she loved fiercely. The girls at her work thought she was twee. She had her school friends over to fill the flat instead, and begged them not to leave. You could see a vestige of that begging in the way she looked at Lyn sometimes. The problem was that Clover was used to being so unequivocally happy: at home, at school, at university. Her school in Buckinghamshire was tucked into rolling gardens. She'd had the sense that the green hills existed within and without the school. Nothing in London was worse for her than it was for anyone else but she wasn't inured to anything. She walked around the city like an open wound with beautiful hair. 'Before George, I'd been thinking that I would just ask my mum if I could spend a year in our house in France. I thought I could get really good at painting or something.'

George was the brother of one of the school friends Clover convinced to stay for a month. She'd invited him and his sister to the house in France for a long weekend and he'd brought Luka. Luka adored Clover immediately. 'This girl,' he would say, and still said. 'This girl. She's a real, actual hippie. So cool.' Before the palest dawning of ski season – and without saying a word about Fourier – he'd coaxed her into leaving London for good. Why not? Being a close few in the mountains was the opposite of feeling lonely in the city.

'We got to her just in time.' The city hadn't ruined her, she was still fresh. She still used 'love you' as punctuation and ran up steps when she didn't have to. She worried sometimes that you could hear it in her laughter, which was gasping laughter that felt like it might never stop, breathless, hysterical in the thin air – that you could hear how happy she was to be there with everyone.

(Elen straightens up when they pull onto the 76. She only relaxes once they've been back on the highway long enough that she understands that they're not even going to ask her to pay for gas. All her things are in a black bag: passport, bank card, deodorant, Vaseline. She has 218 dollars of emergency money in her account. She has one working overdraft and, at a push, two people she can think of to call for a loan. Two weeks' worth of underwear. One week's worth of clothes. She couldn't find her house keys, which she thinks is a little on the nose. The bag is not so heavy that she can't crook her arm.

Almost everything between Bend and Banff is reservation. George alerts them every time they pass a new threshold. 'Warm Springs Reservation,' he reads off his phone. 'This is high desert.' Three hours later: 'The Yakama Indian Reservation. These lands are roamed by an unsustainable population of wild horses.' Four hours: 'The Coeur d'Alene Reservation.'

'Quick,' says Luka. 'Find something to say about that one.'

'In their own language,' George announces grandly, 'This tribe is called "Those who were found here."')

+++

George had never been lonely. He was loved by everyone who made fun of him, popular without being a leader; his upsets mainly manifested in his relationship with women. Even then, he could never claim to be the injured party. It was more that he was always letting them down and then beating himself up about it. He still lived with his parents, just outside of London; he was still thoroughly coddled. His father did something in tech and had apocryphally paid off Google Maps to direct travellers as far around their house as possible. George was unemployed. He was just beginning to find this unfulfilling, and yet was beset by a deep conviction that he was not ready for the working world. Besides, he had a £200k portfolio which he could hear at night, like someone at a sewing machine, working away in the dark on his behalf.

The dissatisfaction was creeping. In wiser moments, he thought that it might be a disenchantment with the fundamental limits of being alive in the world than with anything particular that he was doing or not doing. He saw a therapist regularly and was laughingly blasé about it. The women he let down noted that he was constantly coming up with pseudo realisations – I've been buying all these scarves to fill a void in my life! etc. etc. – and that he was constantly then being disappointed that the epiphany alone had failed to change his cycles of behaviour. He drank a lot and smoked a lot, always just on the outside edge of normal public-schoolboy sociality. He had his teeth whitened and lied about it.

George swam long quiet lengths in his parents' pool every few days. Except for that he was barstool sedentary. There was still power in his build, but as someone who'd played school sports his whole life, he started to enjoy watching his body go soft. Luka and George had been friends for years. George took an adorable pride in the ride-or-die kind of loyalty he saw as a by-product of their class; Luka believed that childhood friendships, forged by privilege, tended to result in him being unable to discard people he'd outgrown. When it was too cold to swim, they went to Val d'Isère. George was a fine skier, but his stamina wasn't what it could have been. The real softnesses were in his habits: getting high before and during, bad eating and tacky behaviour in the après bars. Instead of being sickened by his softness, Luka took George under his wing.

By the time they hit the subcontinent, the old nobility was back in his pale eyes, and he hadn't bought a scarf in months. Obsessed with the idea of a real India, the boys peeped at the outsides of brothels but did not go in. They allowed a real Indian to lead them partway into the Himalayas: Luka said the words 'snow-covered foothills' a lot and noted George's uncomplaining prowess with pleasure. At the top of Kedarkantha when George produced a joint, Luka laughed and acquiesced. The mountains were full of shrines, or cairns. Smoking in the cold of the summit, and with his friend's arm over his shoulders, George noted with blazed clarity the feeling of being saved.

Two months back at home and a particularly bad break-up with a girl who worked in a crystal shop threatened to plunge him back into dissatisfaction. ('One of those dirty break-ups, where for months every new account they follow on Instagram drives a stake into your heart.' Clover nodded sagely. Elen let her forehead bump against the Prius window and thought of her husband running out on her.) So when Luka started detailing his latest fixation, a project with five moons and total personal fulfilment founded on the ideas of an eighteenth-century French socialist thinker, starting with an Austrian glacier and moving from the Americas to

Eurasia – he was very into the word Eurasia at that time – George said yes.

(What nips at her heels, like an unpaid bill or missed call, is that she can foresee what they can't, which is to say, certain failure. What really nags at the back of her mind, like a bill, or a call, or a dress caught in a door, is shouldering the understanding that their Xanadu doesn't exist. They think they're playing at a transience with meaning, and she knows that it's just transience. She knows because it's her coat they're borrowing.)

+++

When Lyn was six, she had wanted to be a ballerina. She was her ballet teacher's favourite student. Her mother told her colleagues that this was because Lyn wanted to be a ballerina in a very adult way. 'Lynny's not interested in the pretty dresses or in being a fairy princess. She wants the 5 a.m. starts, the regime, the eating disorders.' She'd laughed over Lyn's head. It was a winey laugh, Lyn recalled, and sounded like glass. No one else called her Lynny. A few years later, they moved house and the ballet lessons stopped. Lyn moved on to gymnastics, first at school and then with a club in Kensington. Her coach bought her a life calendar – a laminated poster with every week of her life should she live to 100 depicted as a tiny block. 52,000 squares on a page. He put a red arrow just outside the vertical axis pointing to the earliest year she would be able to compete in the Olympics. But when her parents divorced, Lyn's mother decided that the money that was paying for gymnastics lessons could be put to better use.

There was a kind of structure, ambition, discipline to these early routines that Lyn had found deeply peaceful. She liked the uniform. She liked the early starts. She liked putting her body through its paces, being mindful about how she treated it; she liked the idea of body as tool, body as machine. She liked the idea of getting better and better at what she did. (Later in life Lyn engaged occasionally with mindfulness, but not in the soft bohemian way Clover did, not looking for peace or scented candles or whatever. She didn't make a sweet bedroom space for it – she wanted to be able to do it anywhere, on the trains and in taxis; she wanted to not have a wasted moment. She meditated in pursuit of a steely inner force, the same force that ballerinas and gymnasts had.) When Lyn's extracurriculars were taken away from her, the loss manifested as a coolness. 'It's like she hasn't noticed the divorce.' She stopped responding to Lynny.

The peace resurfaced very occasionally, when she was in the mountains or by the sea. Backcountry appealed to her from an early age. Lyn's father was friends with George's father. They went skiing together as children. When they were ten, George kissed her near the mouth in one of the bathrooms of her uncle's ski lodge in Chamonix. *(Lyn recounts this between Hayden Lake and Sagle and the kids in the car roar with the air of having laughed at this many times before.)* She told him that she'd read about someone who fell down the stairs while brushing their teeth and had the toothbrush tear through their throat. When they were fifteen, George's father decided all the children were each allowed half a brandy hot toddy. Afterwards, Lyn and George wandered through the resort pretending to look for cigarettes. 'So you're like a sports dyke,' said George, trying out a term he'd heard a friend at

Charterhouse apply to a netball girl who wouldn't sleep with him. Lyn weighed it up for a moment, her mind on tomorrow's snow: 'Yeah, I guess.'

When she started at university, he told her to look out for Luka. She didn't. Lyn was used to isolation – it was an after-effect of the coolness – and she was very content to be alone. Her friends at university were mostly international students. She liked their studied, easy charm, and the fact that their friendship ended when term did. She met Luka by accident when she was studying in the college music room. He was in the habit at the time of playing long arpeggios to decompress. He couldn't play a single entire piece. *(Elen smiles, caught up in the whole thing; she can't help herself. The Prius cuts through long banks of snow and thin grasses, blue hills sliding round the back of a lake.)*

They found out that they were equals. They went on long walks in the field some way outside of the college and talked about their childhoods and theories of an Old England. It was a romance, in a way. Lyn had inherited ideas of an England luxurious in its rankness. Luka directed her to a TV show written by a president of the Cambridge Footlights . . . He was very excited about it. It cut through dark green Edwardian gardens with Japanese ghosts. They talked about poor England, rich England; lawn cricket, pottery, goblins, gremlins. Neither of them were sure about what they were going to do after graduation.

A year after university had ended, Lyn's coolness was ossifying into a numb thing. She had never thought of herself as a flounderer. Potential futures drifted over her mattress, always in blues and greens. She was obsessively pleased by the idea of a simple life in rural Europe; she applied for a programme which would have had her spending a year on a mussel boat. American rurality appealed much less to her. Lyn and Luka watched the 2016 US election from the Oxford Union where it was televised on roll-down projector screens. Everyone in the dimly lit hall had felt drunk and remote from disaster. For a good time afterwards, Lyn had dismissed white America more or less completely, though she did not mention this in the little red Prius jetting towards the Canadian border.

(They get to the crossing just before evening, stretch their legs under massive swathes of trees and a blue sky. A little later they stop at the Kingsgate Duty Free for cigarettes. Elen looks for a single pack but they're only being sold ten cartons at a time. That's one whim stopped in its tracks, she thinks; but George has caught her looking.

'You can have some of mine, Elen.'

'Thanks, crystal-boy.'

+++

Everyone switches seats so that George can take the wheel. Luka takes the middle seat; he's the only person small enough, except for Lyn. They veer through long roads and the bright cold starts turning darker. Elen notices dandruff on his shoulders. She notes this gently; she isn't repulsed by it. All the same, she begins to consider Luka's disparate unattractiveness. He's not unattractive. The smooth tan, the bright olive eyes, the vigorous smile; of course, he's not actually unattractive. But: next to the rest of the kids, their height, their mouths, he's missing something. It's weird to think of him curling his lip at George, who is soft but also radiant on a different level; it's especially difficult for Elen to imagine Luka keeping pace one on one with Lyn's taller strides. 'A romance, in a way' indeed.)

England was making them all horrible. Where Clover was noticing an increase in the number of train journeys that were being delayed by suicides, Luka was noticing an increasing desire to knock the teeth out of the female comedians when they said insufferable things. But Luka isn't running away from overemployment, or underemployment, or a void of discipline. Luka, it seems, has never really been sad in his life.

When Luka's brother was fifteen, he was making £80,000 a month. Luka was eighteen then. His brother typified a certain kind of excess and Luka didn't want to exist in the same world as it. He started to formulate how exactly he might rebel once he was at college; before that, he had been a Model UN type over-achiever. At eighteen, he was charming in a way that adults often found uncomfortable. Distaste for his child-star baby brother forced him to regularly elect new kinsmen, and he had long been able to make people his own age feel very close to him, very quickly. When Luka was twenty-three, something happened that made it even more important that his new and chosen family found a new world and stuck there with him.

And they are here.

Chapter 10

It's dark when they park the car, a ten-minute walk from the Airbnb. The air is cold and resinous and there's snow on the firs. They shake out their muscles, strap on their bags, make the journey in quiet. Except for Luka, who's muttering little exclamations of amazement at the Rocky Mountains which look like a dead thing in the dark. The website advertises self-check-in via keypad. Sure enough, there's a keypad entrance at the front of the house, but they go straight round the back in single file. The road is banked by tall firs which mostly hide the house from view and the Rockies enclose everything. Elen hangs back as the kids scout out the house. Why is she here? She notes minute, pleasant details – small leaves at the base of a whorl of flowers deep in the grass by the mailbox, a spike of frost on a serrulate fern, a tyre scuff on the wide driveway at the side of the house. She's charged with appreciation, powerful on an electron microscopic scale and brought on by a sudden anxious clarity that they are *doing a crime*.

She wishes now that Luka hadn't been so particularly keen that she ride with them. It's making Elen itch, having left her car behind. She's happy not to pay for gas; she's happy, really, not to put her car through too much trucking about, and she doesn't want to be giving lifts to George every time that he wants tobacco. And when the time comes, as surely it must come, to drive to her parents' place in Michigan, it will be the long familiar drive from Bend. All of these things make sense. Still, the lack nags. It's not so much that all her stuff was in the car – her stuff is cheap, or sentimental, or else with her in the black bag. It's not being able to get out. The teenagers didn't get it: they're from England, where you could get a red bus to anywhere. Elen's glad that they didn't understand. She doesn't want her gestures of trust to be too obvious. She'd also been worried about the car itself. Not wanting to give it to someone to look after, nor to leave it unattended, she split the difference one evening and drove it from behind the brewery to the top of Susannah's road, where she knew it would be safe. It was a shady feeling, driving through the dusk with the lights off and sitting for ages in the car, on a familiar corner with an unmerited anxiety. A precursor to tonight's intestinal apprehension.

The house has more marks of recent inhabitation than the one she'd left behind in Bend. Even the last time she'd seen it – the morning of the day she'd met the kids, the morning she'd returned from the Post Office to find the locks changed – it looked as though it had been uninhabited for months. As though she'd been barely living there. There are plants breathing in the windows here, and a lopsided blind that might have just now been drawn.

The kids are sounding out weaknesses: man-sized windows, a false balcony with the doors opening inwards on the second floor that George bets is unlocked. His beanie is pulled tight over his ears and he keeps forgetting to light his cigarette. He looks like a cartoon burglar.

'The whole frame's timber anyway. Douglas Fir, I bet. Like the doors will give, right?' Douglas Fir is said in the same blithe way that Clover had said 'Oh, are those *navel* oranges?' at breakfast and it pisses Elen off, this need to affirm cognisance of every variant of taste and design. Like they were raised in households where the kind of oranges they were eating and the kind of wood their ski lodges were made out of were decisions to be seriously and joyfully made. Elen's just wondering if she has enough power to call the whole thing off when Lyn slips back into view from around the side of the house. She looks sneaky and bright in the face.

'There was a key under the mat.'

The key fits the back door. They collapse into the house. It's a stone-floor timber building that's stood unoccupied in rural Canada – it's not warm. But it shuts out the chill enough to confirm that it's a real home, a real place, not a haunted abandoned Overlook Hotel wannabe. It's the warmest house Elen has been inside since her own.

Luka explains that they can't turn the heating on, due to the prevalence of smart thermostats. (Luka hates Alexa.) They can risk it with the lights, but first they must go around making sure every window is covered. The kids scatter, draw blinds against the night, cross paths again in the dark of the house and report back. When the lights go on, Elen whistles. It's spare but well appointed. The furniture's wood and leather; here and there are afghans printed with the kind of geometric pattern supposed to recall Pendleton Native trade blankets. There's a bottle of red in the wine rack.

'We should restock it when we leave,' says Elen, and she opens the drawer that every house keeps their corkscrew in.

'Make a note of the brand,' says Luka.

Clover bounces down the stairs. There are three bedrooms, she reports, and sheets in a closet. 'Obviously Lyn and I are used to sharing so Elen, you can have the third,' she chirps. Very smooth. Elen's glad. Sipping the wine as she goes and feeling a bit like a pirate doing it, she joins the teenagers as they settle the Airbnb.

The feeling of *doing a crime* is much less of a problem from inside the house, she has to admit. And the house is beautiful as well, even without the obvious upgrade of not being an abandoned resort. Elen runs her hand admiringly up a wall that isn't peeling. The paper is soft and has a pattern like silk pyjamas. There's a specific damage that cold does to furniture; she hadn't realised it before.

The gritty sediment at the end of the wine comes too fast. It lines her throat like silt. A sexy feeling. An arousal, putting her cold hands all over someone's house. She could hide in their closet. She could run a bath. She could eat up all their porridge.

They colonise the place, set down the cold creams. Elen's unexpectedly thrilled to recognise them: one for Clover's shoulders, one for her eyelids. Non-comedogenic sunscreen. Claus Porto Brise Marine to make Lyn's hands smell like a seagrass that's never existed. They're all unpacking, premature and perfectly; not proper unpacking, more what you do when you kit out a dollhouse, or think about homemaking when you're eight. A pair of slippers tucked under the dresser; perfume in the bathroom; two novels and a notepad lined up perfectly on the bedside table. Lyn drums her fingers on Elen's shoulder blades as she passes. The beat does not subside for a long while afterwards. It runs through her like something biological.

'Oh!' Clover has found goods left behind by past guests in a drawer. She shakes out a bottle of Nuxe golden shimmer. 'Clover strikes gold,' George says to no one. 'I won't take it,' Clover says. But she drips it into her hand and then puts a little on her collar bones, a little on her browbones. She gleams in the stolen light, recalls sun on snow.

Elen puts her bag under the bed in the room they've picked for her; she got lunch on the road but there are still 213 dollars in her emergency account. She closes the door behind her. The bedroom she's been assigned is narrow, clean and colourful. She doesn't have materials with which to make it her own, but that's okay. Anything more than a change of clothes would crowd it.

Being in a room alone seems an unfamiliar privilege. It opens up a new kind of space. The air in it sounds different – stiller, thicker. What should she do? Masturbate? Read a book? Who does she text to say 'I've arrived. I'm safe. Don't worry about me.'? In her experience, being a person who lives in the world includes being beholden to someone. Elen thinks about it and realises that normally the person she would text would be Susannah.

It's unsettling, thinking about that strange and technical

link that had been between her and Robert's family. They could have told her where he'd gone. She's nothing to them now. She'll fade out from even Lee's life and eventually his memory. Aunts and cousins are bigger characters in the lives of children; their spheres of influence are small and intense.

Thinking about where Robert is now, Elen doesn't picture him exploded like before, stirring sugar into a hundred cups. She pictures, momentarily, that he is in one place and that he has a family. A child. It had never occurred to her to worry about that before.

She looks for sheets, makes the bed, steps out of her shoes and her trousers. It's too cold for anything else. She slides into the bed, disturbing her arrangement of the covers as little as possible. The fresh sheets feel unbelievable. Elen has the urge to cry.

She used to make a point of never thinking too hard about who she is. It can be difficult to know who you are when you're not spending time with people who are like you, and Elen stopped spending time with people who were like her basically as soon as everyone her age started having children. She could never be sure if that tightening of her circles had been deliberate or not; some of those women frightened her.

When Susannah became involved with the Bend Fish Passage Advisory Panel, a few years before she got pregnant, it was suggested that the committee was a substitute for having a child. Susannah would explain that it was not a committee, it was an advisory panel. If you wanted a committee, she would say, you could have a look at those silt picketers. She was referring to a small movement who wanted Mirror Pond dredged, the dam creating it impounded, and the Deschutes River to run unobstructed. Susannah was very clear that there were wild differences between the dredging committee and the FPAP. In her view, they were warring factions: one dedicated to destroying heritage and one to preserving life. She would get frantic talking about it. What people don't remember, she'd say, was that when the river ran free, children were always drowning in it. She'd picked up her son and held him very tightly, as though the river were even now extending brown tendrils towards his little ankles. Yes, Elen can admit to being afraid of becoming a certain type of woman of a certain age.

Still, it's natural for a sense of identity to fluctuate in isolation too. These teenagers – Clover, George, Lyn, Luka – are at an age where they should constantly be questioning their selfhood. Elen's never seen less adolescent confusion in her life. Their total self-possession is surely contributed to by having surrounded themselves with people who are alike, affinitive. Attractive and athletic; rich and too insular or self-absorbed to be troubled by it. So what are they doing with Elen; what do they need from her?

There is something watching her stretching out in the bed. She spots it, out of the corner of her eye. Something in a long white nightgown, bending in and out of sight like a candle flame. Elen holds her breath so that she doesn't do anything stupid like cry out or talk to it. Has it followed them from the empty resort? Has it followed her? The cold air in the room multiplies. Why would it make itself known now? No. The spirit must belong to this house. An Airbnb is not a home that has been vacated. It is designed to be passed through. The flowers are artificial, the wall art is carefully neutral. But Elen knows that this was a home once. She can sense it, most likely a family home. Elen turns her head infinitesimally slowly towards the watcher. It is only the light from the hallway caught in her water bottle on the table.

Shock and laughter bubble up in her hard. What a shame, she thinks. Luka would love it if we had our own ghost. He'd probably try convert it to Fourier.

But her heart does race. How to sleep in this ghostless place? She pulls the covers up to her chin like Grandma Wolf and scans the room, counting everything she can see until she feels tired. A framed painting, flowers and a few guidebooks on a shelf. She'd noticed something on wheels under the bedframe – a pull out drawer or a trundle bed – and lying in bed, she thinks she can feel that all is not solid beneath her. There's that electron microscopic power again that comes with this foreign house: the ceiling is composed of a thousand small crests of paint except in two smoothed-over places; a tiny thumbprint of something green and glittering is visible on the corner of the bedside table. Sleep begins to soften her shoulders. She draws one hand out of the covers and rubs at the green stuff consideringly. It doesn't budge. Elen has seen this somewhere before; it takes her a few moments to identify it as glitter glue and so just before she falls asleep it occurs to Elen quite suddenly that this was once a child's room.

+++

The rituals of the next morning unfold easily. There's the automation and anticipation of a first day at school. In early quiet they slip into thermals, mouth at the luxury of having a kettle, slip tea made right onto the table. Elen borrows Clover's deodorant, which is aluminium and paraben free, and Lyn presses her nose into the ski jacket fabric just above Elen's shoulder. 'Yep, you smell aluminium free.' Elen feels very warm.

It's still dark out on the bus. The sun comes up as they hop off, and rises while they walk for a half hour. The snow banks here seem fuller. George smokes. Then, without making much of a thing of it, they set off: a perfect long descent in near unison. The paths they leave behind intersect undramatically. Elen, shaking off the tiredness, comes alive against an unbelievable mountain view. I am lucky, she thinks. It's not something she thinks very often.

She's good as well. Power and ability course through her. She copies George's little hop turns, though they're draining. They forget to eat. After thick white hours they can no longer ignore this and trek over to the occupied faces of the mountain to find a restaurant.

When they arrive, having passed from an unpeopled peak across an untracked spur, the sudden protrusion of the restaurant looks weird. Elen can't put her finger on it – it interrupts somehow. Wall, panes, concrete, glass: the appearance on the mountain of these synthetic materials seem inexplicable. Clover had once said that she'd been overwhelmed in London by the proliferation of manmade stuff. (It pressed in when she was feeling low, the inescapability of it: of metal, of paper, of lampposts, bollards, litter, screens. There was no uninterrupted space; even in the parks, she said, each tree was circled by an individual iron fence.) Elen's happy to be in the restaurant – she lines up for paninis with the other skiers and is glad of the warmth – but she recalls Clover explaining the great shudder of relief she'd had, finding an uninterrupted landscape on the slopes, an endless landscape. Elen can't help it, she's still charmed by the memory of sweet, sensitive Clover recounting how the tension had left her body. Solace in the silent places that can only be reached on skis; in Europe, *Soldanella*. Little things – conkers, pebbles, shells – were never adorable or trinketry for her: they were grand sweeps of emotion, the large in the small. '*Someone has said that the death of a mouse from cancer is the whole sack of Rome by the Goths*,' and that someone was probably Clover.

'Hi there.'

The voice comes as Elen is spacing out by the plastic coffee stirrers, thinking about Clover and conkers and the death of a mouse from cancer. She's not tired but if she closes her eyes, she'll fall asleep. She stands over the coffee stirrers for a long while, as if bewildered by choice.

'Hi there,' the voice comes again.

'Sorry.' She moves out of the way.

'Oh no, I'm sorry, I didn't mean to make you think that you were between me and the sugar packets. I just wanted to say, well, hi there.'

Elen looks up. There's a man smiling in front of her. He has blue eyes and a worn, tan face. He's about Robert's age.

'Well. Hi.'

'Snow's beautiful today.'

'Sure is.'

'Have you been having a good time?'

Elen blinks. 'Sure.'

'You're not staying at Sunshine Village, are you?'

Dread begins to climb her legs. They are found out. 'No,' she says, and looks around for the teenagers.

'That's what I thought. I've been there for a while myself, it's pretty empty this time of year. Oh, I'll let you get back. It's just not so often that you see such a pretty face right at the top of a mountain.' He smiles again, very kindly, and Elen understands suddenly that she is being flirted with and doesn't stop herself from smiling back.

'Well,' she says. 'What a nice snack break I'm having.'

'Oh, for sure. You want me to buy you a coffee?'

'I'm all good, thank you.'

'You ski a lot, huh? You look like a pro.'

'A lot recently. Before that, not at all.'

'It's one of those things that's always there when you need it.'

'What about summer?'

'Did I say always there or did I say always there now? You've got some good skis with you. Good touring skis. You and I, we're the same.'

'Are we?' says Elen.

He nods, and his eyes are shining. 'We get it, you and I. It's all the babies who stick to downhill skiing. Its motions appeal to them: they are grand dramas and tragedies in action. *Niederkommenlassen*: "letting oneself fall down" with all the undertones of suicidal fall.' He doesn't stop looking at her. They're bright, his eyes, and dark, and suggest an excellent power of sight. 'But backcountry – touring, I mean – that's about life. Skis aren't for going fast. Skis are for travelling. All these rope tows and chair lifts, they cheat you out of the good stuff. You never get to see what you're passing.'

Elen feels loosened up, invigorated. She's run off to a different country, far from family or home, and maybe she hadn't thought too hard about it, maybe she'd only complied with the agents of change that had appeared around her. But maybe it's working. Maybe, the relief, the solace that Clover found, is hers for the taking. She thinks that she might respond with something unambiguously flirty, just for the hell of it, *I find you fascinating* or *Let's live* or something. All at once Lyn is right behind them. The blue-eyed man moves aside to let her through.

'I'm sorry,' Lyn says to the blue-eyed man. (She doesn't sound very sorry.) 'We have to go. My friend's coffee is getting cold.'

'It was nice to meet you,' says Elen. She follows Lyn back to the table in unstoppably high spirits. 'That was rude.'

'Oh. I didn't think you'd want him bothering you,' Lyn says.

'No, you were right. Thanks.' Elen finishes the coffee, grins at her rescuer. 'Shall we head off?'

They look around. Clover's in the bathroom. George and Luka are engaged in conversation with a group of boys who look like they belong to a fraternity. It's a conversation that's been going since the queue for sandwiches.

'Ah, he's found some new converts. I don't know what the point of this off-piste shit is if we're going to be bogged down by other people.'

'Guilty,' Elen says.

'No, not you,' says Lyn. She turns. Elen thinks for a second that they could kiss. 'Come on, I'm not waiting for them. Let's go.'

Lyn opens the door for her in a casual way, looking down at her phone in one hand, the other arm aloft for Elen to duck underneath; Elen feels like a spoof prom queen. Robert never held the door open for her in his life. There was a video on the internet which had nearly killed her with laughter, of a girl doing a social experiment in which she didn't move from the passenger seat until her boyfriend opened the car door. Elen had shown Robert and they'd laughed at it together but then she'd thought, Huh. Why shouldn't she expect that? She doesn't like to think of Robert but she thinks of him now; only because of Lyn, only having brushed under the inside of Lyn's long strong arm (the smell of cold cream and Claus Porto travelling briefly past her).

Of course feeling softly towards someone is always a process of comparing – at its best, it's like, oh, this is it, this is the real thing, I've never been in love before! and at its earliest, it's watching out for signs like, oh, I'm not going to be delusional this time, I'll be prepared if this one doesn't work out. Comparisons to Liberty come easier – partly because Robert is such a raw wound and partly, Elen suspects, because she finds it easier to compare liking two women than liking a woman and a man. Not that she 'likes' Lyn – Elen's not a teenager. She just doesn't have much experience of feeling softly.

They don't have chairlifts to set a closing time but the light dictates how long they have. Over their few weeks of skiing together, the teenagers have transmitted to Elen a kind of frenzied feeling that comes towards the end of the daylight hours. A sense of having to speed up, cram in one last descent, drain what can be drained from the remains of the day. She's confused, consequently, when Lyn drops into a sitting position right at the top of a perfect, abandoned run.

'It's a new mountain. Let's take a moment,' she says to Elen, quite softly.

Elen eases down beside her. The cold will get her like this, she thinks, until Lyn pulls a hip flask out of her jacket.

'I thought you were a purist.'

'This is Bombardino.'

They pass the drink in silence. The sky's four or five shades are fantastically distinct. Nothing bleeds: the evening's cloudless, the lines of rock are sharp all about them. Things begin lighting up in the distance, maybe Banff, maybe Canmore.

'You handle your alcohol very well,' Lyn says out of the blue.

'Well, I mean, this tastes like cinnamon.'

'No, but. You drink a lot, I mean.' She doesn't mind being indelicate, Lyn. It's the most American thing about her.

'I don't drink a lot. I don't drink before five.' They haven't seen her drink before five. And actually, she's been drinking less and less regularly in the daytime since her adoption by the teenagers.

'I just thought hangovers were supposed to be awful once you hit thirty.' Lyn passes the flask with a smile and Elen realises that, incredibly, she's being teased.

'I'm a heavyweight,' she says. 'Heavyweight champ.'

It's spring, fully. Slopes are white and green bivouacs under the moon. Everyone joins them after a while, five pairs of skis stood up at rest in the middle of nowhere.

'It's been a good first day.'

'No making toasts on the mountain.'

'I was just going to say—'

'No making toasts on the mountain, Luka.'

'I was just going to say I think we should do some acid.'

'Oh, that time of year, huh?'

Happy quiet white and green. They sit cross-legged in the snow but each one of them has the sense of dangling their legs off the mountain, as off a kitchen countertop.

('This reminds me of India,'

'I was just thinking that.')

There's a small rip in one of Lyn's layers. Elen watches her move, leaking down. Like snow in a quiet town.

+++

Over the next few weeks they ski Cascade Valley, Castle Junction, Moraine Lake Road and the Great Divide. They commit several days to each trailhead. Nearly nothing bad happens until Lyn thinks she might have sprained her ankle. The difference between Hanneke and the overgrown resort is everything: warmth, light, beds, tap water. Knowing that the door is closed.

Chapter 11

The same day that Lyn nearly sprains her ankle, Elen gets lost. It happens like this: the people she knows are all around her and then suddenly they're not. The terrain is steeper than she'd expected, she's going faster, she makes a wrong turn somewhere and she's lost. She steps out of the skis and sits down next to them. She swears. She's just thinking that whatever happens, she'll have to regroup with the others herself – it's not that this face of the mountain is such an unmappable wilderness, but it's quiet, and if some ski patroller does happen to find her, they might want an address or something – when George's shaggy brown head appears, far enough above Elen that she might almost be able to retrace her steps back to him and to where she'd come from. Before she can shout to him, he's hopped the snowbank. He falls quite a distance, lands plumb on his skis and is making his way towards her with enthusiasm.

'Now we're both lost.' It's a scold, and sounds like one.

'Lost in the mountains ...' says George in a sing-song. 'This is the issue with backcountry.' And then, seeing that she's serious: 'How lost can we be? The only way is down.' It sounds oddly like a threat.

*

She gets back into her skis and they follow the declivity through trunks and stems and unusual snowcrusts. It's like following north, George tells her. You can't really go wrong.

Occasionally they come to a steep drop and a view. These are beautiful, naturally: wide expanses of sycamore trees, more snow, wide sky, but they echo a perilousness back to her. Elen scolds herself now, for feeling uneasy. She's only thinking that way because he's a man. It's not like he radiates threat, sexual or otherwise; he's friendly. And he couldn't get away with it (he would surely get away with it). There are just those little things, as they pass between the firs together, that remind her he's a man. A laugh that tends to bray; his thick red hands on the ski pole. Elen remembers the way she and Robert would playfight, and how when he held her down she couldn't believe the difference in their two strengths. That was a long time ago, actually. The memory is tender like a bruise when she presses at it. Anyway, it might as well have not been playfighting.

'It's kind of beautiful being lost, right? At such a height.'

'I guess I've never been lost anywhere as nice as this.'

'Not just the views though. Like, the state of being lost. When you lean into the experience of not knowing where you are or where you're going.' George brays again. 'I sound like Luka.'

'No, I get it. I suppose it's kind of the aim of the game. Your game, at least.'

It would be called a ski accident when George killed her, Elen thinks. It's not implausible at all. It's the opposite of implausible. (There has always been darkness and hurt, and then there have been mountains. But Elen will find

that darkness and hurt follow her even into the mountains.)
Hadn't she thought herself it would be an easy thing to do
when she'd hiked the Cascades in April? Susannah's yappy
friend. The ravine. Oh; or was she thinking of Robert, in fact,
and of the cyanide in apple seeds?

But George is talking. 'Did you see that?'

They've been surrounded on all sides by wild, perfect
beauty for so long that Elen isn't sure what he might be talking about. Perhaps this will be where she turns her head and
he clubs her.

'I thought I saw something move in the trees. Huge. On
foot. Too big to be a skier.'

Elen laughs and doesn't turn her head. 'So then what?'

'Um, you ever heard of Bigfoot?'

'Bigfoot, Jesus Christ. I think they call him
Sasquatch up here.'

'Yeah, perhaps. Okay, I'm not saying it was Bigfoot, or
Sasquatch, but there have always been things that are uni-
dentifiable and spooky living in the mountains. It's the same
as the bottom of the sea.'

'You're joking.'

'Cryptids.' He picks up the pace as he continues. Elen
weaves alongside him, working on not thinking about how
long it might be before she can eat. 'They're big on lake monsters in Canada, I think. When we were in Argentina, it was
the Iemisch. Japan has the Ningen. Oh, Elen. The Ningen is
fantastic. Giant, sub-Antarctic thing that lives in the sea and
scares whalers. It looks like a ghost.'

'Sounds like a Greenpeace scam.'

'I want to stop by Mount Ararat when we go to Turkey.

There's good skiing there, I think, and some big old weird plesiosaur descendent.'

'I think we're making progress. I want a hot chocolate,' says Elen, trying not to sound like a kid. In reality, she's not at all sure they're making progress. The part of the mountain they're struggling down has begun to form a kind of ridge, leading around its side like a helter skelter. Not an exact path, nor a ski run, but perhaps a route trodden down by animals.

'We should take this,' George says decisively. 'This will actually take us round to the car.'

'I'm not sure. I think the car's over that way.' Elen points. Then she puts her finger away, realising it looks ridiculous. Over the past few minutes, a cloud has risen suddenly; or they have walked into a cloud. The views have disappeared, the beautiful wild: everything but each other and the ground a few feet ahead has been obscured by opaque, vaporous white. George is already following the ridge.

'This is, just, definitely the way,' he says. 'I remember it from the map.'

'I don't want to end up on the other side of the mountain. We don't have cab fare. I want to go straight down and then walk round.'

'No, I swear this is quicker.'

Elen stops protesting because she can feel that if she did, she would begin to whine. She feels reduced to kidhood despite herself, following along sulkily like a child walking behind a parent, close to tears and unable to match their stride. Which is to say, a teariness brought on by dependence as much as discomfort. It's the physical that's breaking down her fortitude. Her heel pulls away from her ski boot on every descent and then rubs when it rocks back into it. Her skis aren't as good as George. She could kill him. With a ski pole, she thinks. He is not thoughtful. Although they are still going downhill, more or less, they're not skiing so much as stepping, setting the skis down one at a time for vast portions of the track. Elen's knees resist in their sockets. She'd thought she was getting stronger, but this doesn't feel like that.

George turns around, suddenly excited. 'Dyatlov Pass,' he says, in a thick Russian accent, swinging his ski pole.

'That's a great accent,' Elen says, her throat closed up. She's reminded of Robert again, of the last moments of strained levity before a big fight.

'Dyatlov Pass. It's fun to say. Dyatlov Pass. Dy-et-lov Pess.'

'What are you saying?'

'The Dyatlov Pass incident,' he says, increasing his pace. 'It was this skiing expedition in the Ural Mountains, in the eighties or something, where a group of skiers were killed by a cryptid. Or exposure to a Russian chemical weapon, but probably a cryptid.'

The cloud makes white misty tendrils Elen can touch. They turn into water on her jacket. There's a glee in George's voice that reminds her of him back in Bend, whistling, holding a scaffolding pole.

'Nine hikers, I think. And every single one died. It was snowing mad, freezing. The kind of weather where nothing could have convinced you to leave your nice warm tent and sleeping bag until the sun was back up at least. And yet something happened in the middle of the night that had them cutting their way out of their tents in the dark and fleeing.' In the fog, Elen can't tell whether he's looking back to check her response. His voice seems to be coming from far away. 'The Russians concluded,' he says, 'that the deaths were caused by a "compelling natural force."'

Their path is becoming more certainly downwards. At the next turn, they begin to come out of the cloud, although it remains unclear to Elen whether or not they're on the car-side of the mountain. Perhaps we will die up here, she thinks. She could bite her tongue off from tiredness. But they're able to ski rather than step again, albeit slowly.

'Dyatlov maths,' George says, in that same stupid voice. 'Dy-et-lov meths. Nine hikers. Six died of hypothermia, three of physical trauma. Four bodies were found in running water which, of course,' – he looks quite serious here – 'rules out vampires. Two bodies missing, one missing a tongue. One missing eyebrows. At first, patrollers only found the "remains of the small fire under a Siberian pine." That's straight from the Wikipedia page, but quite poetic.'

'I wonder what we'll be missing when they find us,' says Elen. She points at George – 'tongue' – and then at herself – 'ears.'

'They tried to blame it on the Urals' indigenous people, obviously, but the bone fractures were not compatible with external injuries. Elen. They literally could not have been caused by a human.'

Elen can feel that they are closer to ground level, to food and humans and away from high cliff edges. The perilousness should have dissipated. But George keeps talking – bone fractures and missing eyes and Russian monsters, cryptids pacified by offerings of wild animal meat – in his level, jocular voice and she keeps one eye on the needlepoint of his ski pole. Until, with the other eye: 'I can see the trailhead!'

'Hell yeah,' George says. 'I bet Clover's waiting for us with your hot chocolate, bless her.'

Elen turns to him. She hasn't been thinking about her heels or her jarred knees for a while now, she realises. Not since he started the Dyatlov Pass story. They're whizzing quite fast towards the end, hopping the bolts of gorse that lie in wait under the snow.

'You know you shouldn't have hopped the bank like that,' she says. 'There was no need for you to get lost. I don't think you're a very good ski-squatter if you're putting yourself in danger like that.'

He bray-laughs. 'I had to come get you, Elen.' He goes on to say something like *You're not that good of a skier*, instead of *No man left behind*, but still. She could have hugged him.

+++

They all take the next day off because of Lyn's sprain. Of course, Lyn disapproves of this massively, but Elen is feeling suddenly at peace. She's having one of those days where you thrill at doing everything very slowly. Set each foot down deliberately, feel Hanneke like a tree root under your soles. Fill the kettle. Close the lid gently. Carry a netted punnet of peaches from the fridge to the table, feeling with each step like some kind of country maiden. She might smoke one of George's cigarettes.

Lyn's been minimising her sprain or playing it up, depending on her mood. At dinner yesterday she'd rolled her eyes so hard when anyone mentioned it that Elen decided the fall must have actually bruised her ego. But that evening they'd washed the dishes together, and Elen saw the moment Lyn had been on her feet too long. She looked very pale and her eyes shut tightly.

'Let me take it from here,' Elen had said, and Lyn had looked grateful, childishly grateful, and stumbled down into a chair. That left Elen washing and drying Hanneke's china and sporadically lifting her eyes to where Lyn sat examining her injury. Lyn looked like a girl. Her face was oddly softer than Elen had ever seen it, though her small mouth was tense with pain. The ankle bone bulbed between the long fingers. Elen's chest twanged.

In these moments, Elen finds that the attraction that occasionally springs up between them seems ridiculous. When Lyn's vulnerable, as she is so rarely – perhaps only really when injured or during discussions of her mother – she becomes a person more like Clover, and Elen feels that same fondness that she might direct at Clover and which Lyn seems to fend off. When she feels attracted to Lyn, when she wants that pale hair falling in her face, Lyn is being her opaque, oblique, over-adult self. A self that makes Elen feel ... if not young, then not older. And only a little like a teen with a crush.

But Elen's calm this morning, intentional about small movements. Usually nobody's supposed to hang around the front of the house, due to the risk of being seen, except for a quick smoke, but today the snow is coming so thick and fast that everyone except Lyn goes out to wonder at it. Elen's a little less wowed than the kids but even she can appreciate the snow budding for longer and longer on the wet tongues of the tree branches just in sight. The taste of peach is still in her mouth.

'El.'

Lyn's come up behind her. The shortening of her name is new. 'Found your phone,' she says and Elen smiles before Lyn dramatically limps off back inside. (She's been playing up the injury since last night, as if to undercut the truth of any pain Elen might have witnessed.) Elen retreats into the doorway, turns the phone over in her hands neutrally. It had been mixed up in a hamper of things some time ago, maybe back in Bend. She'd enjoyed being without it.

The kids hardly use their cell phones at all (except Clover on occasion), which Elen's sure has to do with Getting Back To The Land and with Not Being Beholden To Anyone. Lyn seems especially allergic to the idea of being in touch. Back in Bend, over the spread of postcards, Clover had mentioned that Lyn keeps her mother completely in the dark. Elen has seen that borne out a number of times since, if an absence can be borne out. Lyn's phone is never off silent, but when her mum calls she turns the whole phone face down. The calls come regularly, at all times of day. Once the screen light had jarred Elen awake at 5 a.m. in the girls' dorm in Bend; she'd watched Lyn consider the phone. (Her mother hadn't been assigned a contact photo.) A couple of seconds passed before Lyn turned it over, and then she'd looked up and caught Elen's eye. 'I text my dad,' she'd said. 'So she knows I'm okay.' When Elen had asked why she spoke to her father but not her mother, Lyn had told her. 'My dad sends me money, and my mum's a fucking monster.'

She'd held the phone up so that Elen could hear a voicemail.

It was only audible in fragments but the fragments were bad enough. *'A year. A year, Lynny'* ... *'It's not enough to know that you're alive'* ... *'You came out of me. You're killing me'* ... *'You're just like your dad'* ... *'Just call me. Just call me once, Lyn.'*

'She's a manipulative genius,' Lyn had said. 'All this "You came out of me" shit. She used to tell me that when she was pregnant they'd never once seen me in the foetal position, that in all the scans I was laid out completely straight in the womb, like a *bar of fucking iron*, the better to slip right out. She said that's how she knew I wanted out, from Day One.'

Children can be cruel. They're famous for it. As a young child, Elen didn't act out so much as clam up, so her cruellest moments were less along the lines of letting her mom think she'd died and more related to being woundingly ungrateful when she came to opening the Christmas presents her parents had saved for. But she'd thought such cruel things about them. Her whole conception of them had been an operation in cruelty. By the time she was in high school, in love with Liberty, she'd decided her parents were a dull, shit affront to being alive. She stopped laughing at their jokes, answering their questions. When her relationship with Liberty had progressed, her parents graduated from being a pointless, suburban aberration to standing directly between Elen and happiness. Elen stopped talking to them in full sentences. She fixed them with a look that said they weren't worth her breath. She cringes to think of it now. Her mom became awkward under her daughter's unsparing eye: she began to bustle and scuttle and leave a room that had just Elen in it. Her father couldn't put his finger on what had happened so he spoke to Elen with a confused friendliness and retreated for the most part into his wife.

After she and Liberty broke up, Elen had found she wasn't a child any more and she looked at her parents with unchildish eyes and saw what she had done. She tried first to retreat from it and then to mend it, but she was too late. She'd shattered that unnamed thing which is supposed to come naturally to families. Elen hadn't been especially close with her parents beforehand but that year-something of child's cruelty had dispelled the child's notion of unconditional, contractual love.

The drinking and sleeping around phase followed quickly: she'd filled the space of the shattering with things that broke more loudly. After graduation Elen was out of the house as often as she could be, and when her parents didn't say anything about it, she knew they were relieved. By the time Robert found her, she was sure she could be careful with him: it had been ages since she was cruel. When, finally, they'd packed her things up and set properly off for Bend, Elen hadn't cried in the passenger seat. She'd leaned forward until she could rest her head on the dashboard, and she'd pictured her parents letting out a great breath. Within a couple of years they'd fallen out of contact almost completely. It wasn't radio silence quite the way Lyn's mum has it – she doesn't leave them wondering if she's dead in a crack den – but the monthly phone calls had soon winnowed down until they were only at Christmas, and then only at most Christmases. She'd been glad when they'd moved out of her childhood home; it left even less reason to visit.

A fair few years after that, when they were miserable

financially and Bend was as bright and happy and expensive it had ever been, Elen had called her parents up. Not for money help but just to hear them talk – just in case they were able to resurrect that old soothing power. Her dad had answered, sounding equal parts friendly and impersonal. The handset down in Michigan picked up her mother laughing at something else, maybe the TV, and Elen had put the phone down. It was good to understand that there was no bond invulnerable to breaking, not even one sanctioned by blood and law. It meant she could see clearly when it happened with Robert. And, as a child, as with Robert, it had been Elen who was cruel first.

But the teenagers are playing in the snow outside, and Lyn called her El and found her phone and is putting on a limp. She can't call these kids cruel. It would be like calling wild animals cruel. It's just that neither kids nor wild animals are trained to curb their instincts: neither understand that there are reasons not to always do what they want, at least not until someone civilises it into them (in a process conveniently disdained by both Fourier and Luka). What had Fourier said? That a community must be built from 'passion and pleasure'. Its citizens must be rewilded out of curbing their instincts and back into doing what they want. Maybe that's Luka's long game: de-civilising the teenagers, turning them back into children for real, or animals. Lyn letting her phone ring could be down to Luka's evangelising; he might have uncivilised her out of answering it. Sure, Lyn tends to laugh off his Fourier rhetoric, but it's so easy to be convinced that you don't owe anyone anything. It's a conviction Elen's dallied with since 1999.

*

Stood in Hanneke's doorway as the snow comes down, she flattens out her palm as if to weigh the returned phone. Then, with some misgivings, she holds down the power button. The old default wallpaper blinks at her before the notifications flood in: many texts, some voicemails. Nothing from Robert. In fact, almost everything is from Susannah. Elen holds the phone to her ear, skipping through the voicemails. She doesn't let any of them play for more than four seconds until she hears the cool voice of Robert's brother.

She lets this one play, in part because of the small authority he's commanded for as long as she's known him, but also because his voice calls Robert so clearly to mind. The earliest memories ... dull, essential: watching both brothers in conversation and trying to figure the family resemblance; Robert holding her hand, pulling her closer, his brother a few steps ahead, leading the way to a new Chinese restaurant.

The voicemail starts out almost professional. He even introduces himself; surely it hasn't been that long. But Elen can tell, too, when he starts getting into it, though his tone doesn't change. 'I don't know if you left your car on our road to taunt us, or what. But whatever your intentions, it's worked. Lee keeps thinking you're coming home, he gets excited. Suze is worried you're dead. I don't care what you do, Elen. By all means, take off. But it is absolutely irresponsible to cut and run in the way that you have. It's childish.'

Outside, the twenty-somethings are playing in the snow. Luka is whooping. It's ridiculous, Elen thinks – they've been skiing for months now. How can they still be delighted by snow? She laughs despite herself. She was just a kid (which is to say a twenty-something) when Robert married her. She was younger than Clover is now.

No wonder that pulse that flickers up between her and Lyn feels like a teen crush. The last time she'd properly wanted anyone but Robert, she'd been eighteen. Occasionally, since he's left, Elen finds herself feeling physically like she did at eighteen – skinnier, smaller, tenser. Robert's brother has this effect on her too; she thinks it's called a dressing down.

'I don't want to phone the police. But you are, technically, missing. Your parents say that you told them not to expect you.' It rankles a little that he's called her parents. Mainly it annoys her that they'd tell him anything at all. 'If you could just shoot us a message telling us who you're with. Who are you with, and are you safe?'

She looks out the window. The sound from her phone is tinny as though his voice is coming from very far away, or at least a long time ago. There are crackles in the connection like a detective radio in a film. Who is she with? Lyn is upstairs sleeping. And is she safe? Snowballs explode like heads, peach is still in her mouth. Dread knocks on the door, tentative, just two knuckles, as George raises a perfect and enormous snowball above his head. Like in the haunted resort, so long ago, when she'd imagined he'd killed an intruder with a scaffolding pole. When he launches the snowball at Luka, she thinks, There's a rock in the middle. This will kill him. Instead, it explodes like all the others: ordinary, spectacular.

She'd thought of Robert exploded before, into every possible betrayal. Adulterous in Olympia, Victoria, Canada, Portland. He'd cut and run. If being civilised is to be beholden to someone, Robert had been rewilded. Lyn has outrun her desperate mother. Maybe Elen would explode spectacularly too, all over the mountains of Turkey and Japan. A new voicemail has started in her ear – Susannah, speaking fast and plaintive. Elen turns the phone off just as another snowball explodes, hurled by Luka against the front of the house.

Elen starts laughing and can't stop. Raw laughter, nearly hysterical. The kids look at her quizzically.

'Funny phone call?' says Clover.

'I'm sorry, I'm sorry.' Elen drops the phone on the counter, still creasing up. 'It was the snowball. It reminded me of something.'

'Go on.'

She won't say Robert, or Robert's head. 'It made me think of those videos of fruit exploding.'

George shrieks with delight. 'I know the ones you mean! Watermelons bursting in the heat.' He steps up to her. 'Do you know why they explode?'

'Because they're rotten,' Elen offers.

'Exactly! Or, sometimes, because of faulty genetic code.'

Clover looks to Luka, who's looking quite murderously at George.

Elen doesn't even turn. She's stopped questioning Luka's odd responses to popsicles and watermelons: some people just hate strange things. She'd had a friend once with a Lycra phobia. Or fetish? A school friend, from back when she was a kid. Elen only smiles at Luka's face, which is about as threatening as a schoolchild with a Lycra phobia, and steps out into the middle of their circle where the snow starts to cluster immediately in her short hair. The phone is face down, forgotten. Clover wants to make angels.

Chapter 12

So in this house which is a house, not a haunted house, or an abandoned house, Elen finds that their togetherness grows to fill a house shape. The teenagers have always been a well-made clan but in Banff, Elen had felt that she slotted in more as the single, scrabbly constituent of an outer circle. In this house, they move around each other like family. Like friends who have known each other for years. In fact, Elen is reminded in particular of that point in the life cycle of a friendship group where everyone first gets out of school, or out of their parents' home, and starts pretending to be a grown-up. Elen's pretending to be a grown-up too, cheers-ing with a glass of red wine when dinner's laid out.

+++

George tells them that there's no need to celebrate his birthday; no one could top his twenty-second, which had been Bread and Circuses themed with performances from an authentic ringmaster.

Elen's more than ready to take him at his word, but Luka's been up late three nights drawing sketches of an ambitious cake for someone else (Clover) to bake. She watches them, secretly pleased that slope-time was cut short for birthday prep. A strain is unfolding, like a long hand on her left thigh. Then, a long hand in her hair – a real hand, gently tugging a bunch of Elen's short hair backwards. Lyn, of course. 'You and me. We're being sent into town for the feast.'

It snows the whole car ride there. Weird that it should feel so cold inside the supermarket, Elen thinks. She watches peacefully as Lyn manoeuvres the trolley, not quite sure why she's here. True, Lyn eats more for fuel than pleasure (calories are energy and energy is freedom, she says, bullish, whenever Clover looks discontentedly in the mirror) but still, she knows the drill. She knows the codes: which is the pleasing granola, artichoke, tomato variety, coffee strength. Elen thinks that her part is mainly to stop Lyn getting bored.

'At the last party,' Lyn begins, eyes on the children's birthday cakes, 'George got so ruined that he had to be put in a cab at eleven. The party was at his house, by the way; he was just so insistent that he couldn't stay there he was put in a cab around the block. I met the crystal girl at that party for the first time. George's ex?'

'What was she like? A real hippie? A Wicca woman?'

'Mainly she was just stunning. I mean, antisocially beautiful. Do you know what I mean? The kind of attractiveness that makes you feel bad about yourself for days.'

Picturing Lyn feeling bad about herself for days, Elen is bewildered. Not just because it seems that Lyn lacks a normal adolescent anxiety or even (almost) a normal degree of human emotion. But also because – 'You know you're very beautiful, right?' She hopes that she doesn't sound motherly.

Generally, Elen finds that compliments mean nothing to Lyn but this one stops her in her tracks just for a moment.

'Um, yes,' says Lyn. She resumes pushing the trolley at a pace; Elen's somehow offended her. 'I know. Not in a big-headed way, like, at all. It's not important to me, or anything. But it is just something I know.' She snatches up a pack of candles. 'It would be silly to pretend otherwise. I was scouted for modelling once, you know.'

'Wow,' Elen says, sincerely. Lyn's face drops. It might be the most sudden, most dramatic expression she's ever made; she seems sincerely horrified by the words that have come out of her mouth. She wheels hurriedly round a corner and says, 'We need to get cambodge seeds apparently. What? You know George. It'll be some recipe he picked up in India. Or his ayah used to make him.'

'Huh?'

'I'm joking.'

'Can you tell me what's happening? Have I upset you?'

'No. No,' she tucks her chin into her chest, stretches her neck out. 'I just didn't want to tell anyone.'

'What do you mean? About being beautiful?'

'About being scouted.'

'What? It's fine – I asked.'

Lyn's face remains full of a subdued horror, which confuses Elen because Lyn is always talking like this. She might be oblivious to compliments but, consciously or not, she is constantly saying things that act to delineate how special she is. ('When I was born, I had blue eyes. They changed colour three days later.' Or: 'Some people say that girls born under the sign of Sagittarius are the most beautiful girls in the world.') Long ago, her grandmother had told her that white flowers had bloomed outside the hospital the day she was born, and Lyn had held on to that for some time.

Now she sighs, some kind of brown pod in one hand and flaked almonds in the other.

'I never wanted to tell anyone, because every girl who gets scouted then can't shut up about it. It happens way more often than you'd think. And even the girls who are like, sorry, no modelling for me, I care about my education or whatever, bring it up at every party. It was a point of pride for me, I guess. God, I didn't even tell my girlfriend at the time. It's better to be principled than to be beautiful.' She smiles with a rare wickedness. 'Even better to be principled and beautiful.'

Elen keeps a straight face when Lyn says the phrase 'my girlfriend at the time'. This is a code, too, although quite a different code from which is the correct granola. Elen knows because she's had to do it herself so many times. It's an ancient cipher that roughly translates to 'I like women'. Elen would later find out that the 'girlfriend' wasn't formally a girlfriend, so to speak, but whatever; it's a necessary by-word, one that you have to manipulate whole conversations oh-so-subtly to include. Perhaps the modelling story had never even happened. Impressive if so.

Elen asks dutifully about what had happened to the girlfriend and Lyn tells her. She talks as they pass through the supermarket and head further through Banff towards an old fashioned sweet shoppe, where they buy yet more birthday surprises. She's still talking when they switch from the sweet shoppe to the Banff Cannabis dispensary. (Kids, such kids.) Lyn's tone throughout the conversation is not the tone of someone imparting secrets; if anything, it's the tone of someone surprised to find herself talking so much. It had ended badly, she explains. They'd been competitive exes. It had ended strangely.

There's a lake near Lyn's house back in England, only a short walk away. It's one of those beautiful, deep lakes with thick brown water, not dirty, but full of a healthy silt. They'd swum there often; it was the backdrop to a lot of their happiest memories. Being so deep, the lake is cold even in summer, so when they'd started swimming there together they'd had to train their bodies to acclimatise, going in for thirty seconds on the first day, a minute on the next, until they could stay in for half an hour at a time.

'It was nice,' says Lyn. 'Like we were calibrating our bodies together.'

Elen looks at her. It makes sense that Lyn was a swimmer. Sometimes she does that stretch where you put your hands behind your hips and pop your chest out, which makes her look like a swan, or like somebody who's waiting impatiently. The muscles across her shoulder blades flicker suddenly into prominence; a muscle in Elen's chest moves to match them.

It's funny to think of Lyn and Liberty's similarities. Liberty had a swimmer's back too, broad and muscled. Elen swam with her once, no lake, just laps of an East Lansing community centre pool.

'Anyway, we had a lovely relationship with this place, obviously,' Lyn continues. 'Virginia Woolf used to go swimming there. We'd swim, sunbathe, whatever. She was super strong. I think she's training for a pentathlon at the moment, actually.' (Elen winces.) 'She knows how to shoot, which is quite hot. But it's just one of those things ... You can be so compatible with someone on the surface. After we broke up, we saw each other at the lake all the time. It wasn't a question of whether or not we could have avoided each other. Even if we had managed to avoid each other, I hated the fact that she was out there telling people, like, "Oh yeah, I love wild swimming." Like "Oh, Keillor Pond? I swim there all the time." It was such a petty feeling, but so strong. Totally proprietorial. I was like, I introduced you to the pond. But she thought her connection was stronger because she'd been the first to be able to stand the cold long enough to swim a lap. It was ridiculous. On the one hand, the lake's nearer to me, we always walked from my house, but on the other hand she's read more Virginia Woolf. It's ... how do you possess a lake, you know?'

Elen nods seriously, closing her eyes like she's meditating on possessing the un-possessable. 'Division of anything after a break-up is going to be fraught,' she says. A nightstand, split open in a skip; a brown front door belonging to no one. And as an afterthought, 'Was it your mother's house? The one by the lake.'

Lyn parks the car in the usual spot. 'Yes it was, the fucking witch.' They walk the ten minutes back to the house in quiet reflection, carrying four bags of birthday goods between them.

During the first seven minutes of quiet, Elen wonders whether to use the ancient cipher herself. She can't figure out what she would say to Lyn about Liberty, although they do resemble each other in a few specific ways, swimming aside. For example, Elen has a vague idea that her attraction towards Lyn is rooted in covetousness, but is not simply covetousness. This had been the case with Liberty as well, even if the things coveted in each instance were very different (cold cream & a Moncler jacket & a real copper tongue scraper & youth & total self-possession . . . vs. long brittle blonde hair & a natural, comfortable femininity). There are things that Elen and Lyn have in common that she's sure Liberty could never have understood. For a long time, Elen had thought that she could do without people, that she didn't mind being alone, that she liked it even. She's no longer convinced that's true, but it's a conviction that she recognises in Lyn's utter self-sufficiency.

During the last three minutes of quiet, Elen wonders who she's been framing these ideas for. Who is she in dialogue with? Who's her narrative partner? She is that person for the teenagers, sometimes. She let them try out their speeches about the mountain that Noah might have crashed his ark into, or old girlfriends and deep lakes. She's permitted to hear out Lyn's mum's plaintive voicemails in order to validate her cruelty, and to corroborate that Lyn leaving means something, that it makes someone sad. She observes their escapades. She acts as a human record. Elen thinks that her relationship to the teenagers is the same as the way that a postcard says I Have Been Here. They engrave their genius adventures by having her witness them. Their conversations with her are intended as a general pronouncement: *do you see me? Isn't this fun?* And when she nods, it is fun. Private but public, a message for all disguised as a message for one, like a postcard that slips unclothed through the postal system and is handled by dozens of people to whom it is not addressed.

+++

The party hasn't quite started. Elen is more than happy to put a wash on in Hanneke while Clover bakes a cake under Luka's direction; she's glad in her bones to have a machine stream warm soap through her thermals. This is until the birthday boy careens past her and drops a T-shirt over her shoulder, red with some kind of marinara. 'Can you just put that in with yours, please, Elen?' he calls, already halfway back up the stairs. Elen stares into the gridded circle of the washing machine. How weird. Of course she can put this T-shirt in with her wash. He's not asking anything of her, really. They all pitch in, with dishes, cooking, getting groceries; why does this half-task specifically feel like a throat punch?

She's pushing with her thumbnail at the lumpy surface of the stain when it comes to her. In Bend, Elen had been responsible for the 'linen service' that they'd offered the people who'd rented out the garden room. The guests were in and out of the house all the time – there was no toilet in the 'guesthouse', so they used Elen's bathroom – and she'd kept the shed clean, threw away their fallen tissues, but something about the linen service had felt gross to her. 'Maybe it drives home that it's hospitality and not real estate,' Robert had said. She didn't know. It was like handling the winding sheets of every invading body. One hiker (who'd kept her sports sunglasses on for the duration of her stay, meaning Robert and Elen at no point actually saw her eyes) had handed Elen her dirty laundry still warm. There was a big reddish stain on the bedsheet. Too dark for marinara. Automatically, Elen started to scrape the surface of this stain with her nail until she realised. No big deal. Mothers everywhere, etc. But it had made her darkly angry.

There was nothing to do about it because there was no getting away from the fact that the guesthouse had saved their lives. Elen could still remember the desperate enthusiasm with which they'd converted the garden shed. Two potted plants on the side where the painting had gone wrong. They were making Bend work for them! They were like those tanned twenty-year-olds who made tourists pay thousands to be taught how to water raft for two hours! The only furniture they could fit inside it was a bed but Susannah gifted them some ugly appliquéd cushions as well as the fairy lights, both of which drove the price right up. They'd tagged it as 'glamping'. Neither could believe that anyone would pay to stay there; the room was three by three metres. But people with money love to experiment. (Look at Luka, trying on a squatter's skin, chatting about hunting rabbits for dinner.) And when it started working, the guesthouse was like deliverance, because feeling like the poorest people in the happiest place on earth had started to become unbearable. Everything in their own house had been looking like something they could sell to pay rent. That third or fourth year in Bend, Elen had originated an ability that she can still call up at will where she could look at anything – photo frames, desk lamps, spare tyres – and see it as its resale value down to the cent. The ability is still accompanied by the feeling that her stomach is digesting itself.

She wonders how broke the teenagers think she is, exactly. How poor did George think she was when he threw his T-shirt at her? They know she's homeless but that could have been nothing more than an accident of the break-up. After all, they'd met her as an (ex-) resident of the 'Your Vacation is Our Life' city, and something about Bend plasters over the actualities of being poor or unhappy. The kids probably thought that Elen could have lived in Bend for nothing like them, spending all day out in the mountains and then catching fish from the sea for dinner: fun and food for free.

Elen puts a laundry capsule in the washing machine. She has been holding the box for minutes. Her throat is still tight. She puts in another capsule. Then she puts in another.

She'd been twenty-two when they'd moved and seen the cockroaches racing all over the floors of their new house and understood. Sure, there'll have been cockroaches in the million-dollar mansions in Awbrey Butte, but these ones were fat and insouciant. 'This is your life,' they skittered. And a couple years after they'd arrived in Bend it started showing up on lists of Top Places To See, or Small Cities With Highest Quality Of Living, and the tourists multiplied ungovernably, and coffee started costing four dollars fifty. Elen realised fairly quickly that they were surrounded by too much desert to drive anywhere cheaper. She sipped her beer and watched the cockroaches flicker over her bathroom floor. Only after the guesthouse could they breathe easier, sleep through the nights again. But Robert had run off with that money, not that there was so much saved.

The clothes are just colours swirling in the drum now, arrhythmic, soothing. Elen doesn't remember closing the machine door. She wonders when the ghost-host family decided to rent their home out to tourists. There's nothing desperate about Hanneke, nothing that says last-ditch life-line. Elen's not quite sure what to feel for them. She's pretty sure she wouldn't give a shit if someone had broken into her guesthouse while she was away, as long as they'd left it nice and tidy. But it was something more than red marinara on a white shirt that had reminded her of linen service. Teenage tourists in other people's houses. Elen is a postcard again, a souvenir they'd picked up, watching inert as they make themselves at home.

+++

On the inside of cards that close, the teenagers have written lovely things to George. Unearthed memories and sweet, well-crafted wishes. Elen gets drunker than the rest and goes to bed early while they stay up late with no one except each other to watch them smoke Banff's finest cannabis.

Chapter 13

An Isolated Incident

All of the curtains and window shades in Hanneke must remain drawn. There are many (the lopsided blind at the window where Elen first spotted a plant from outside the house, the drapes in her room which let through a knifing draft, the tattered wicker roller blind of the bathroom window) but they don't require attention. A curtain only has to be drawn once. Despite this, the windows are a constant source of low-level paranoia from Luka, a chink in his chill facade.

One morning, Lyn turns up the corner of the blind in the sitting room window to check the weather. Luka snaps, instinctively shouts at her to drop it. Elen notes the moment of fear passing through the room, impressed. George has frozen over his cereal. No one knows how she'll respond. After a long silence, it becomes clear that this is the response: a stillness that could be blithe or could be seething . . . Those cool eyes! She holds the stillness until it becomes clear that Luka has to diffuse the situation, which he does by using his fingers to scissor open a space between two of the slats and peeking through it like a cartoon spy: 'You have to be subtle, Lyn, like me.' All the same, no one touches the blinds after that. The windows are like locked portals in the wall. (Elen finds it strange trying to keep track of what's behind which window. If she thinks about it too long she gets all turned around.)

The darkness doesn't take a toll since they're out all day. By the time they're done skiing it's evening, and the kids are lighting their candles with pleasure. Only the mornings are made strange – dim, crepuscular, slightly sad. Low white light purls in through the front-door transom and creeps soft over mugs of tea. Elen says sorry to the water-bottle ghost when they leave her behind with the lights off and window shades drawn.

They're at dinner when they hear a car pull up to the house. It takes a moment to compute all the implications of this everyday sound. But the car has pulled up unmistakeably off the road, past the circle of fir trees, basically up to Hanneke's front door. The engine is still running.

'Fuck.'

Clover puts an empty glass over the candles in a bewilderingly smooth move. The instinct, of course, is to take a look through the blinds, but that would be impossible.

'What the fuck should we do? Hide?'

'Let's not panic,' one of them says, panicked.

'Americans,' says another, 'have guns. And get violent.'

'We're in Canada.'

They hide for what feels like hours. Elen's holding herself crooked behind the stairs, thinking: will she be the one they call ringleader? The adult, the American? Is that why she's there – have they brought her as a foil? The car engine stops. Then, eventually, it starts up again and they hear the car leave.

Luka motions them out.

'Do we think those were the owners? Do we think they're coming back? Do we think they might call the police?'

'Maybe it was just people off the byway. Maybe they needed to turn around. Or, like, make a call.'

Their plan of action is instituted immediately, and frantically. First, they put the house back to how they found it. The towels are hidden back away, the beds denuded, the cutlery restored to its drawers. Within half an hour, Hanneke is returned to the impersonal and hospitable state in which it had appeared when they first broke in. Entropy who? Next, they begin packing their belongings back up into suitcases, ready to go at once if necessary. It doesn't take Elen long. She zips her black bag and tucks it under a chair, taps her foot against it. She's at a loose end for a while, watching the kids put the trappings of their loose life away. She feels very disconnected from them. The skis are in the car, except for Lyn's which she's heaved back to the house to wax. They hide these like a body.

Luka plots a way out round the back and makes it clear to the others (he stops just short of imposing a fire drill). The beginnings of a mutiny here, which might be a real problem, except that in general the state of emergency has inspired a happy sense of obedience. For twenty minutes, however, Clover stands her ground, arguing that they should leave immediately. Obviously! Hanneke's family might be on their way back with a whole host of Mounties. Elen surprises herself by agreeing. It feels weird, voicing her objection to Luka's plan, given her relative newness to the group. Sweetly, Lyn, Luka and George all disregard her complaints in exactly the same manner as they had Clover's.

Although, eventually, they accept that the car's not coming back, they do not sleep that night. Paranoia lingers like vapour or a tapeworm. They are still not allowed to lift curtains – the imperative is greater than ever – which means that the outside is unknowable and the threat therefore constant in their imaginations. They are also forbidden to: turn on lights, run hot water, make loud sounds. It's like not living. It's like being a ghost. For the next two days, every time they come back from the mountains they are breathless to find no one in the house. Elen checks under her bed, feeling stupid. It takes three days for their belongings to start accumulating on the surfaces again. It takes four days before they're at ease.

+++

In the middle of the third night, Elen slips out of bed and pads quietly down to the kitchen where, in spite of instruction, she turns the sideboard lamp on. An intruder at the kitchen table! The shriek catches in her throat when she sees that it's only Clover.

'Thanks for the light. I wanted to put it on. I'm still quite freaked out, to be honest. That spooky little car.'

Elen catches her breath. 'I'm the same,' she says, and sits down. 'It's not too bad in the daytime, but you do think about it at night.'

'Thank you also, by the way, for agreeing with me at the time, that we should leave right away. Like, maybe their way has now been borne out, but we were the only ones thinking sensibly.'

'Well, if we get found out, you all go back to your parents' but I don't know what I do.' She looks at the side of Clover's head. 'Maybe I go back to my parents too.'

They make tea and toast, sit quietly: the comfort formula has never lost its efficacy. They watch Hanneke's cold air turn to moisture on the surface of the kettle. Clover's eyes glaze over a bit and she jumps when the toast pops. When they've eaten, Elen asks her what she's thinking about.

Planting trees, she says; gardening in the grounds of an English stately home that had been long given over to the National Trust. Elen imagines the warm glow of acers and borrowed gloves in frost-hard soil.

'Sort of. At my old job they made the new hires do it every year: one day of tree planting to register the company's charitable arm. I thought it was pretty fun until someone was like, yeah, do you know we also finance the beef producers responsible for razing millions of hectares of the Amazon? I felt guilty the whole autumn.'

'Oh. What made you think of that?'

'You know why we were on the same page? About getting out of Banff as soon as that car pulled up?'

Elen chews the cereal thoughtfully. 'We're realists.'

'Maybe. I don't know. I think you and I are looking for a future in a way that the others aren't.' (Elen raises her eyebrows, prepares to be patronised.) 'I'm going to try and make sense. Luka loves the idea of this, right? His travelling community, it's important to him. But it's not the solution to a problem. If Hanneke got rushed by Mounties tomorrow, he'd go home, have a sulk, maybe try again in a year. But we need it.'

'Why do we, particularly, need it?'

Clover has often been described as an empath. She doesn't like to rest on her laurels, she tells Elen, but a new understanding has dawned on her, like inspiration. Gravely, she tries to explain it: how she'd grown up with the unshakeable surety that she lived on a planet which was unthinkably big and that there was no animal with a mouth wide enough to eat it; how this surety was suddenly cut out from under her, debunked by the increasing seriousness of global warming as presented in news reports and school assemblies; how the future of the planet was revealed to be finite, at worst apocalyptic, at best unknowable; and how what had happened to Elen, with the vanishing husband and the house, had to have been a trauma of the same nature.

'It's your contracted future, disappeared. Life as you know it disappearing. That's why we wanted to get out of here, quit Hanneke, preserve the group. Lose the battle, win the war, whatever.'

Maybe it's the 2 a.m. but she's getting agitated. Sleeplessness has its fingers in her brain, thinks Elen. She's a sweet girl, Clover, with her adorable, grandiose fear that she's living out the end of history. Elen can't laugh; it sounds too familiar. The analogy had been minimising but correct: the atmosphere was the same at the end of a marriage. Dwindling oxygen. Inevitability. A premonition that, whatever her next step, no foothold could avert the conclusion (of love, or life on Earth). Ten different things to have for dinner, one in-escapable outcome.

Now, in Banff, the End Times feeling still creeps up to Elen on occasion, just with a different name. These days the doom arrives as the sense that the preordained dissolution of their ski clan is due any moment. How can it be true – skiing and carefree for ever? Can it be true? It's the dual cognition of the magic trick every time. Something crazy and fantastic is happening and you experience it and respond to it and the hairs on your arms stand up but at the same time, even while you're sitting there in the dark, another part of your brain is trying to understand it intellectually, trying to find the false compartment, the secret door.

'There's this condition called solastalgia,' Clover's saying. 'It's like, a kind of anxiety caused by environmental change. I think of it as feeling homesick when you're still at home. It's usually diagnosed in people after natural disasters, volcanic eruptions: they're still at home but their home is unrecog-nisable. I know, right, how could I possibly relate? Which, you're right. For me it's just the sense of end times, I guess. Global sadness.'

'Homesickness while still at home,' says Elen. 'I know the one.'

'It's a real rich person's disease. Like latching on to any-thing. Hypochondriacs who end up mimicking the symptoms of people who are forced to leave their homes. The guy who originated the term solastalgia said that it "uncannily" resembled symptoms of displaced Navajo.' Clover closed her eyes, remembering. 'Disorientation, memory loss, depression, homelessness, estrangement from self. No one thinks George and Lyn and Luka are displaced peoples; they're all homesick for an era, a Britain that never existed, a Troy. But I miss what's here now – I get sad at the inevitable loss of things I can currently touch, if that makes sense. Oh, I don't know. Does it make sense?'

Something about the warmth, the mug warm in her hands, the dim light from the sideboard, something about Clover being overtaken by the feminine urge to caveat, stops Elen from laughing at the rich person's disease. 'No,' she says. 'It makes sense. You're anxious about the future, of course you are, there's so much of it.'

'Yes! Luka says the problem's modernity. My dad says it's a phobia, like sharks, or the dark.'

'You're anxious about the future,' Elen says again. She touches Clover's shoulder tentatively. 'And you're shaken, because of the car in the drive and the Mounties. But it's going to be okay.'

Clover exhales. She finishes her tea, leans in to the touch. The calm in the low-lit kitchen builds and swells for a minute before she breathes out and admits the worst, most selfish part. What scares Clover more than the end of the world is the idea that she won't be able to have a baby.

'I've had broody spells since I was fourteen. But everything, *everything* says it's unethical to have kids right now. We've hit critical overpopulation, overconsumption, uncertainty. It would be a burden on the system, but also it would be a horrible life for the child. So I take Luka's weird chat quite seriously because it's the only way – to imagine that there's a future in which we've created something safe and sustainable and lasting.' Clover takes a breath. She's been too excited – she lowers her voice. 'Do you think that's terribly regressive? The family house is the utopia, blah blah.'

The drop in volume means that Elen's had to listen closer. She's been caught up in it for sure: understanding the reasons for Clover's commitment to the gang of runaway utopianists, and how deeply, convincingly she feels them, has lifted a weight off. If she could figure out why Luka's so devoted, perhaps she could begin to consider this a longer-term solution; at the very least shake the sense of predestined failure. She thinks of the coin disappearing in Luka's hand. Magic's just a swindle that you've agreed to. Clover is still waiting for a response.

'It's not regressive,' says Elen. 'It's a human need. Look at all the stories we tell about how scared we are that something will happen to our home. Goldilocks breaking and entering, the pigs' houses getting blown down, those kids eating up the candy house. D-I-V-O-R-C-E.'

Clover nods seriously. 'I just can't have a baby in a world where there's no such thing as snow.' She looks over to the kitchen window to see if even now there might be snow falling, but of course the blinds are all the way down and must stay down.

+++

They never do find out whose car it had been, or what they'd wanted. Like so many things, it feels irreparable when it's happening: a trauma, a blight, the end of the world. And then it's surprisingly forgettable, until it's nearly nothing.

Chapter 14

When Elen reflects on the car incident, she has trouble remembering details. How long they were hiding. Whether anyone had seen the car at all. She can't recall at all the actual feeling of the fear, the weight of it: only that she'd felt it and then not. Perhaps it's contagious, she thinks, the Lotus Eaters syndrome of the young. They just bounce back, don't they? Once she saw her nephew eat a nail. Lyn, Luka, George, even Clover for the most part, all still have that assurance that vanishes the tiny problems. They move on blithely and don't look back. Even Elen's small uneases (strange sounds at the haunted resort, George throwing a snowball, a car pulling up to a house that should be empty) are smoothed over by their forcefield of irrepressible optimism. They are hypnotically efficient hedonists. They are still that well-oiled machine that rolls on in the pursuit of pleasure and which will not let anything catch in its rotor blades.

+++

Sometimes the kids will peel off into strange discourses, seizing on pointless things in a way that feels rehearsed and artificial. Maybe it's cabin fever, maybe it's a private joke, but these spiels always take Elen by surprise and remind her of their otherness. It's as though they've each been tasked with bringing an interesting talking point to the table; Luka spends two afternoons trying to verify a story about a ski lift in Livigno, a two-man chair running from Mottolino, opened by the last Roman Emperor. He says that he doesn't want to retell the story if it's a myth. ('But you'll rim Fourier?' says George.)

One evening, in the car on the way back, they're talking about squatting rights. Talk comes around, as it so rarely has, to Elen's eviction. Did she know that she could have stayed in the house with the painted nightstand? Luka asks. He doesn't say 'the painted nightstand' but she is thinking of the little flowers on it.

'You could take them to court even now,' he says. 'There's a girl in Brooklyn living in a townhouse that's not hers with a one-time Airbnb host who can no longer bear her and she can come and go as she pleases because the one time the host tried to change the locks, the court found in favour of the guest for, like, years.'

They're all nodding, all in on it; George helpfully grabs his phone and adds that 'The party seeking title by adverse possession may be called the *disseisor*, meaning one who dispossesses the true owner of the property. Cool, huh? The seizor.' They're googling, googling.

Clover, strapped in next to Elen, taps her knee and mouths, *Are you okay?*

'I'm fine,' says Elen. She doesn't need to stand sentry to an empty house, a long-dead relationship. She has new muscles! She's watched her body change.

*

But when they get back she retreats to her little room and she's glad to have it to herself. The black bag's under the bed and there are 168 dollars in her account. She wishes she hadn't put money in for George's birthday dinner. The conversation has knotted up into her like something worked into a paw. It doesn't ring true (surely she could not simply have stayed in her house?) and so it's not worth thinking about. But the wind has been knocked out of her. They have it so easy and they are so unselfconscious. They should be a million times more self-conscious, she thinks. They should be embarrassed by what they have. Sometimes it only takes a moment for other people to seem disgusting to Elen. It's written into her, the thing of having been alone for so long – these two months without Robert but longer than that, years longer. It's fibrous in her wrists and fingernails, the needing to be alone. These four, their constant talk, their loud, braying laughs, are rubbing her raw, eroding the protective layers of self-possession that she'd accrued in solitude. She can hear them downstairs, clearing the table, bouncing a rubber ball from some arcade push machine back in England. They'd laughed, telling her about its mythical origin, as they laughed at and mythologised the origins of all things – wood (silver forests), oats (Oman), navel oranges (Valencia), each other's parents (Norwegian royalty). Oh, she can't stand it. They're playing some kind of beer pong, presumably an antique version learned at the headquarters of some underground society. The girls were the worst. They shriek. They shriek for the boys, the boys honk for each other: Elen lay on a kid's trundle bed, eyes focusing and un-focusing, immobilised and hating them. *I hope something explodes for them,* she thinks. *I hope the ball takes eight eyes out in a series of ricochets.*

She pictures their heads exploded easily. An ear, perfect, hanging on the kitchen hooks where the mugs go. Two skulls indistinguishable having collided across the table. Everything else – the shrapnel of teeth and cheekbone and cool unblinking eyes – flat on the walls.

She rolls over, thinking a little wine would make everything more valid, or she could sleep through dinner and wake up the next morning, when her community would be back to feeling house-shaped again. Luka knocks on the door of her children's room before she can decide. Elen thinks she can hear the ghost skitter back behind the water bottle. *Disseisor.* Dispossessor. He lets himself in.

'So, I've been thinking ... Well, I wanted to say that I've been talking out of my arse. I've been doing way more research on squatter's rights in the US – like, that's all I've done for the last hour or so. And I'm sorry. You can't appeal your eviction. You knew that, of course. A bit idealistic, but mainly quite irritating from us. I'm really sorry, Elen.' He seems sorry, deeply, frankly. She can tell that he'd planned a whole new life for her. She gets up awkwardly and hugs him (which he adores, wrapping his strong little forearms around her).

'Shall we go skin a rabbit for dinner?' he says.

Downstairs it turns out that he's not really joking. 'I think it will be self-actualising,' he says, tugging on Clover's skirt.

'Luka, if you catch and kill and skin a rabbit, I'll cook it.'

'I'm not eating it,' says George. 'We're not going full *Walden*.'

'"I love the wild not less than the good."'

*

Luka cooks by himself tonight, rolling jacket potatoes up in tinfoil and talking unstoppably about what tomorrow might hold. The others have dissipated but Elen listens, sipping at a warm red wine. The hood lights above the stove are slipping around in the cradle of her hips. She thinks of the blue-eyed man bending her over into the sugar packets until Lyn comes to save her. But what she says is, 'How can you always have them with you? What about airport security?'

'The thing is, girlie, is they're literally paper. It's just squares of paper with a tiny, tiny bit of research chemical splashed on to it. Or something. It's like transporting a perfume tester strip.' Luka straightens up. 'Can you tell George that dinner will be ready,' he says, with his hands on his hips and looking quite matronly. The differences between squatting in a highly equipped Airbnb designed for guests and a totally abandoned building are many, and one of the salient differences is those little soft furnishings put aside for tourists – towelling robes and the beautiful King of the Grill apron into which Luka is currently tied.

Elen moves around the house leisurely. She calls George's name, straightens a vase on the table. She goes to her room, or the child's room that has been designated hers, to grab another layer. George and Clover are in her bed together. It's impossible to misconstrue. Her beautiful hair is wound up in his hand. And her breast, definitively, is in his mouth.

She considers turning around but they've seen her now. George nearly falls off the bed.

'I'm sorry – I was just grabbing a jacket.'

'Oh my god, Elen, don't be sorry! It's your room.' Clover looks like she'd be about to leap up and give her a hug if she wasn't covering up her nakedness with Elen's bedspread. 'We're sorry.'

His back is pink and freckled. He looks like he might laugh.

'No worries.' Faux breeziness. 'Get changed and then you can take it on up into the boys' room. Oh – Luka says dinner's ready.'

George speaks. 'Elen could you ... avoid mentioning this to Luka? I don't want to put anything on you, but. Please.'

'Okay, of course. I mean. Would Luka mind? It seems very natural to me. You two make a good couple, actually.'

'No, no, we're nothing like that. Oh, I think it would just bother him, you know. Unnecessarily.'

'It's the group,' adds Clover. 'He'd be worried about damage to the group.'

'Yeah. Of course, none of my business. Don't worry about it.' She snags the pullover she came for. The movement – two fingers over a hood on a hook – feels over-delicate, trite.

'We'll change the sheets,' Clover calls quietly after her.

Elen can't put her finger on why, but it feels like something terrible has happened.

Chapter 15

She's shivering outside Hanneke. She isn't supposed to be stood where she is, out at the front of the house where Clover had made snow angels and where, not long ago, a stranger's car had appeared and disappeared. The snow is thick on the ground. Luka, George and Clover are huddled, squatting a little way from her. They've formed a circle around something but Elen can't see what. There are no tracks that lead to them, she notices; it's as if they've materialised from nowhere, or been dropped in their circle by something airborne. Elen looks down at her shoes cautiously. She lifts one leg, then the other, sets them softly down again. The snow does not keep the mark of them.

From inside the ring, Luka laughs loudly. It's such a familiar sound. He's holding his phone aloft. Straightening up, he reads aloud from it. 'Okay, wikiHow says: "Kill the rabbit humanely. There is no need to allow the animal to suffer. Respect its value to you." Quite sweet from wikiHow, no?'

Clover chews her lip. She doesn't seem to see Elen, who moves in closer. George, who has his back to her, drops into a kneel and now she can see what's in the centre of the circle: a young jackrabbit, shuddering between the ground and Luka's hands.

'Kill the rabbit humanely,' Luka repeats. Now Elen sees the knife block sitting in the snow outside the circle. It's been there the whole time. It isn't the knife block from Hanneke's kitchen; in fact, strangely, it's the knife block from Elen's house back in Bend. (She can tell because the knife handles are in different colours which are supposed to correlate to the food they're best suited to cut.) She doesn't say anything, but Clover's already seen the block and is passing a knife over, the chef's knife with the blue handle, meaning meat.

Even kneeling, George's back should block the whole thing from view. The angles are all wrong, Elen's too far away, but for whatever reason she can see every move and moment. Luka keeps one hand flat on the rabbit's twitching back in a way that reminds Elen of sex. With the other hand he pulls the knife along the rabbit's natural seams: across the grey choke where head meets body, lightly down the belly. The animal spills open with a red force disproportionate to the cuts. It snaps from living thing to unrolled meat with no transition. The blood blooms oddly on the snow. Where did the fur go, the skin? Clover has it in a long soft skein. The fur is totally clean of blood; she winds it round her hands into a handwarmer. 'Guys, does this make me look like a little Russian lady?'

No one chases Elen when she starts to run away; they stay gathered round the flayed red centre of their circle. She tries to work out where she is but the geography eludes her – she's in Banff, she's in South West Bend, she's a thousand miles from any town. Remember, it's just that children are cruel! (The mother cries her eyes out on the phone and the daughter plays the voicemail for a stranger to laugh at.) They've only found a rabbit for dinner! Clover only wants to cook it up into a fucking cacciatore! It doesn't matter, actually, what town is nearest to Hanneke because once Elen's broken into the ring of fir trees that surround the house – have they always surrounded the house? – she remembers that they go on for ever. The ring of fir trees is a forest, or a country. Like any idiot in a horror movie, Elen's surprised to find herself where she's been all along: a cabin in the woods.

+++

Of course, Elen wakes up in a child's trundle bed in Hanneke rather than a sinister forest shack. A rosy light pushes through the curtains as though to hammer the point home. Usually those kind of dreams don't disturb her too much; she's been mountain dreaming for weeks. Before that, during the two months after Robert left, when the drinking was at its heaviest, she'd felt basically inured to nightmare. As long as her brain's throwing up the scary stuff while she's asleep rather than when her eyes are open, it's nothing to worry about. Still, unlucky that the bleeding rabbit corpse should appear to her right before today of all days.

George has scheduled the drop for nine this morning, which means that they should be coming up about an hour later, somewhere near the top of Mount Norquay, and fully tripping by the first descent. He's clearly the one who knows the most about this kind of thing. He divides the tabs with a pair of silver sewing scissors which make no sound – it really is a very well-equipped B&B – and everyone puts about two thirds of a tab on their tongues just as they head out the door.

Not everyone; Clover declines. She doesn't want any, which George says is ideal, really, since she can be the tripsitter and clear-headedly handle anything that goes wrong. 'Not that anything will go wrong,' he adds.

Elen parses out the conversation with new and forensic concentration now that she knows what she knows about George and Clover. (It's much more fun to think about than nightmare-Luka grinning while an animal bleeds out.) Is that why she's not partaking? George does not seem any more nervous having been found out. If anything, there's a sly, conspiratorial aspect when he addresses Elen, as though he were expecting a fist bump.

There has always been a weird sort of comradeship between them. Elen had noticed early on, back in Bend, that George talked to her in a different voice to the one he used with Lyn and Clover. At first, she assumed that this simply reflected the lack of appeal she held for him sexually. She was not flirtable; she was no longer Girl and therefore she was neuter. But it wasn't quite that: it was a knowing voice, a nudge-y voice. She thought then it was perhaps akin to Luka's general joshing: respect for his elders combined with welcoming her to their clan. She only realised where the voice was actually coming from one recent night in Banff when, at dinner, George had been talking about his ex, the crystal girl. (In retrospect, Elen wonders if this kind of thing hurt Clover's feelings. Is it negging? Or ghosting, perhaps?)

'She's batshit,' he'd said. 'She can only sleep on her right side and she told me it was how the stars were aligned.' Batshit, he'd said again, looking at Elen and Luka like, girls, huh? That's when she'd worked out what it is, the flavour of his friendship, without him having said a word straight to her.

She'd seen it before, in Lansing, Michigan. Guys love having that one lesbian friend. It confirms their coolness to themselves. Back then it was something that got them off, too, but she's pretty confident that's not the case here. Strange, coming from this rich joker. Not the sentiment, but that he's sniffed out her butchness. Without her telling anyone, he's found that part of her.

She listens to his slightly dopey voice as he continues talking totally neutrally about Clover's decision not to drop acid. He says that the best part is that they'll have a designated driver, since no one will want to be walking their skis home from Norquay at the end of the day. Elen watches Clover driving, one hand on the wheel, casual, beautiful, not apprehensive at all about her passengers turning into bloodthirsty hallucinators. She will take her cue from Clover. The tab has been disintegrating on her tongue for twenty minutes now. There can't be many visions left to leak. She chews, swallows.

George and Luka talk excitedly – too excitedly? *Are you guys feeling it?* – about past trips, friends' trips, a boy who dosed up at the beginning of a fourteen-hour flight to China. Elen contributes very little. She mentally rehearses how to ski, motion by motion. She gathers information, also, concerning the relative experience of the teenagers. George is an acid expert. Luka has taken it a few times. Lyn never, but she was once well-versed in some other hallucinogen. Perhaps it's an English thing, or generational, but Elen hadn't realised the youth of today were taking so many drugs. They're out on the mountain now, and Elen is feeling something. It's a short climb, a long traverse, then a longer climb and the snow is pricked through with sprigs and yellow gorse. Once the boys start talking about drugs, they can't stop; they confide in her as if she's someone's cool mom. 'Calvin Klein is coke and ketamine,' says one. It's an addictive disclosure, reliving how cool they were at university to this unruffled American who would, they imagine, never have expected it of such clean-cut good skiers.

She starts getting visuals towards the end of their ascent. The mountains either side of her join in the middle of the sky in a striated cloud which is also chemtrails which are also a starling murmuration. Which are also starting very slowly to look like Greek letters.

'Look,' she says.

But it's too late, for they've reached the point where acid ceases to be social.

It's impossible to articulate what they are thinking. Nevertheless, with half-started sentences Elen attempts to acknowledge the sensation that what they are thinking is the same. She remembers the secret – Clover's whole breast like an egg in George's mouth – and thinks that they all know, that every called name is a reference to it. Luka says, 'Good one, Clover,' meaningfully and about nothing in particular, and Elen starts. 'He knows? You know?' Lyn points to her hand in response. It says ACID on it in letters which are bleeding into her skin in a toxic-looking way which might also be forming the Greek alphabet. Oh, right. Nothing to worry about.

Unexpectedly, although she is apparently 'pranging out' about little personal things, the skiing itself is fearless. She worries about a man at the base of the slope who looks like he's filming them, worries that somehow her period's started and is leaving marks on the snow through her suit, worries that there are insects crawling up her skis, but does not worry about the skiing. If there were any likelihood of her falling into other people she would 'prang' about the necessary disentangling, but there isn't. This is firstly because on acid the clear line of the route pronounces itself to her. Then this is because she is suddenly almost all alone.

The mountain rings with quiet. An actual ringing sound, delivered psychically into her head.

'Do you hear that?'

Lyn nods.

'Does acid produce aural hallucinations?'

'No,' says Lyn, 'that's real.' She looks at Elen, unsmiling but sweet. Her eyes are still clear, no longer cold. Her face looks like it's about to soften. For one second, her mouth lengthens into the shape of Liberty's. A little thrill, a little plughole feeling in Elen's stomach. They are close. They are too close. Elen, having just mastered the incredibly abrupt turn-stop, has used it to park a hair away from Lyn, sending snow spray all over her legs.

Lyn puts her gloved hand over Elen's on top of the ski pole. The mountain rings louder.

'We,' says Elen, panicking, scrambling, 'we need to find the others.'

'They're down there,' says Lyn, with an indecipherable expression.

'No, you don't understand,' says Elen, thinking that she can't leave Luka alone with Clover and George and their egg-mouth secret. 'I have to,' and she skis down and of course forgets as soon as the air is under her.

The forgetting is a big part of it. Their ascents take ages because they're all so befuddled by beauty that they forget they're supposed to be moving in any one direction. The scale of everything is bewildering. And it doesn't make Elen feel small, it makes her feel massive. On long traverses they come across all sorts of what Clover labels grandly *the alpine flora of the Rocky Mountains*. They glide by leaves like bandages on low tufted plants, a larch with purple scales; they adore the forward motion; they stop to laugh at the flattest fir tree anyone has ever seen, hanging its broad low head like a dog lying down in the snow. Elen sees George staring at one of its fingers and knows that he can see what she can – the whole world in the needles clustered round a fir cone. If she stares enough at any serrated plant, its little curlicues would begin to form Greek letters.

'Why is it always Greek letters?' says George, quite unprompted.

Elen wonders if she's skiing over buried things. The tracks behind her move, spell words which she passes too quickly to read. They move harder when she looks at them; it's a sort of power.

Lyn calls something into the air. A hiss, a shh. Luka and George pick up the call. *Schuss*. They sing it like loons and Elen follows them down. A cold fastness between her thighs again. George disappears. Sober Clover disappears. Lyn disappears. Elen can't see where they've gone and she's moving unstoppably fast – her soul's been left ten turns behind her body. Luka howls at her and she tumbles to a stop. He zips down to her and helps her up. 'Elegant.'

'I thought you were screaming at me to stop! I thought I was about to fall off a cliff!'

'I was screaming at you to stop! You have to look at this.'

He makes a gesture. The point at which she has come to a stop is, in fact, majestic. Vistaed white and green; bare, full of blue sky. It's gutting. He shrugs like *I didn't want you to miss this.*

Elen looks at Luka. 'Did you really jack off to the thought of a mountain?'

'Absolutely I did.' His smile encompasses the whole wide world.

They hold hands, descend in tandem to where the others are waiting.

Lower down the mountain they spot dozens of indistinguishable brown birds, fist sized. Lyn can name them all. Elen loses everyone again and then hears Luka talking about a phalanstery with spires and courtyards, of course, of course, and turns the corner to see him and George, beautiful, familiar. George skis off in a blur of colours. Elen vacillates between the sudden understanding that actually most of the effect of acid is just that of a moving coloured filter and the feeling that it is much, much more. Her body is constantly falling through the air; she feels like she's skiing even when she's not skiing. Maybe acid is just skiing in a tab.

She grabs Luka, who is standing by himself, and shakes him. 'Acid is just skiing!'

'I KNOW,' he sings back.

The whole way home is a series of imagining that the effect has worn off and then having it flare back up again. Clover

hums tunelessly along to something on the radio. It is a surprise; Elen would have guessed that she could sing beautifully.
Something about being in the back seat, something about the
warmth of five bodies: it's making her feel very small again
and when they get out and troop into the stolen house it is
with a sense of coming home that she hasn't had since she was
a kid. It's warm, their home. She's been feeling like a kid all
day; little rather than teenage. 'I got married at twenty-one,
did I tell you?' she says, two, three times. Everything before
the marriage was such a long time ago. She would have to go
back to being nineteen, eighteen, twelve, to be a person with
no memories of him.

The teenagers investigate the Airbnb through the fading
acid lens. The colours on the afghans glow; Lyn opens a
drawer and picks through the silver. Only Clover is hungry
('You don't really get hungry on acid,' says Luka wisely) but
they sit around her meal companionably and drink beers with
her to no avail ('You can't really get drunk on acid').

George sits by the fireplace, playing a song. He can't light
the fire, in case someone sees the smoke who shouldn't, but
he'd found a space heater in an upstairs closet and they gather
around it in the place of a fire. Elen listens to the song, plait-
ing the fringe on the afghan with cold, chapped hands. Even
as the words set off the usual chains of emotional memories
of her own tenuously related experiences, she is aware of
a sudden, separate consciousness of what the song itself is
actually about. That is to say, for a few seconds, she understands the story of the song as is told in its lyrics, without any
extra inferences or associations on her part. The song – not
that it matters – was about a cowgirl, on her own outside

of a marriage for the first time, going to the club. Elen fills with a vague nostalgia for the way one could listen to songs as a child and hear them just as the stories they are, and live in the stories of them (*Matty Groves* and *Tam Lin*), without the songs prompting associations unstoppably. Getting older reveals itself to her in this moment, with the fraying rug in her hands and the ferns going silver outside, to be nothing more than becoming a collection of sensitive threads which when touched, even lightly, provoke hard feelings. The threads themselves are an accumulation of loves lost, feelings unacted upon, friendships forgotten, resolutions unkept, or tasks at which she hadn't tried. It's unbearable. She is full of undone things and she feels that if one of the teenagers even brushes her as she contemplates this she will burst into broken glass. This evening, listening to Miley Cyrus's 'Midnight Sky', she is reminded of the way that she once listened to music, the way these kids still do. This evening, Elen recovers her ability to listen to the song and the song alone, which is to say, her ability to love without grief.

Chapter 16

Elen wakes up feeling like a child. It's a good feeling. They're all nestled up among the blankets, the ashtray is full; a board game pulled out of nowhere has been taken apart and its pieces gleam in the orange morning light. The soft comedown of the night before has not yet dissipated.

Something like love warms in her. Luka's sleepy head rolls about on one arm of the sofa; there's eyeliner on one of his eyes. Lyn is curled up on the floor, one leg stretched out for the cold slate. Elen unfurls herself. She's great at taking acid, it turns out! The butchered rabbit dream was perfect bad-trip material and it hadn't occurred to her once. She decides she'll look for George before she puts the coffee on and pushes into the girls' room, the child's room, the boys' room. All empty. The worry is that she's going to stumble upon something evil again. Pink freckled back, tit ovate in mouth, blue-handled chef's knife. But then, back in the sitting room, there is Clover, sleeping soundly.

Luka opens his eyes. 'Hey family. Big night, no?'

Elen's making coffee. First, though, she taps Lyn's cheek very lightly and, having ascertained permission, slides a cushion underneath her blonde head. Luka smiles at this, lets it pass uncommented.

'Clover, coffee?'

A muffled no. She opens her eyes a few seconds later. 'I like your eyeliner, Lukey.'

'Where's George gone?' Luka asks nobody in particular.

'I thought the shops maybe.'

'Maybe he's gone to that nice café to get us some delicious croissants,' says Lyn without moving from the floor.

A couple of hours pass, decreasingly companionably. It becomes obvious that George has not gone to get them some delicious croissants. They won't go skiing today, decrees Luka. Soft from acid is the excuse, but really they're manning the fort for when George comes back. Luka calls him. By the fifth or sixth call, he's becoming furious.

'His phone is on. He knows I can hear that his phone is on.'

'Should we be worried?' says Elen. Clover looks up from her lap where she's been locking and unlocking her fingers. Luka shakes his head with some certainty.

'I feel a bit weird about it,' starts Clover. She pauses for some time. 'Just because of him having disappeared after the day you all did acid.'

'You think he might have got into a weird headspace? Freaked out and left?' Lyn says.

'No, more like, what if the acid was still in his system when he left? What if he thought he could fly or something? And like, jumped off a roof?'

'Oh, I've heard that one. Or, he thought he was an orange and tried to peel himself, yeah?' says Luka. Clover blushes and he softens. 'Listen, it had basically worn off by the time we got back. We were skiing on it, Clovey. We weren't trying to peel ourselves.'

'He definitely came back with us, right?'

'People,' says Luka, exasperated. 'He's not in danger. He's just a twat who hasn't let us know where he is. He'll be back before you know it.'

They quiet down for a while. They do not allude to the day stretching out. They do not suggest skiing. They eat bits and pieces throughout the day – a slice of bread, a tangerine – as though if they do not recognise lunch it won't have passed. Whenever Elen looks at Clover she can see the terrible things behind her eyes as though they're floating above her: George in the basement of some Canadian serial killer who likes to prey on British travellers, George mangled on a freeway. Rolled out glass, parts of a car, blood in his mouth; horror stories. After a few more hours, they all go back to their phones to call, text, email him, except Elen, who has never had his phone number.

'It's just irritating, to fuck off and not tell us where he's going. Like it's just not on.'

'He's fine.' Lyn takes up the refrain quietly.

'Yeah, he is obviously fine but why's he left us in the dark? Knob.'

Clover starts crying. Lyn looks alarmed, looks one degree of bewilderment away from patting her on the head.

'Don't cry, C,' says Luka, 'I'll just bollock him when he gets back.' But Elen catches herself thinking that Luka is regarding Clover with suspicion.

Clover decides to bake something. Peach turnovers. It's a bizarre response to stress. Lyn clearly thinks so too, but sits

on the countertops and keeps her company in an uncharacteristic act of solidarity. It's sweet. Elen has come to understand
that all Clover wants is sweet, ordinary friendship, the kind
she has with her girl friends from school. But Lyn can't really
offer this to her, so it was natural that she'd turned to sweet
and ordinary George.

The house is quiet. Clover and Lyn are baking in the
kitchen; Luka is feeding chunks of wood into an unlit fireplace, fuming aggressively and performatively. Without
warning the teenagers appear to have devolved into some kind
of church fellowship. There's no place for Elen here.

She lies in the girls' double bed. It's firmer than the child's
mattress in Elen's room, and the sheets smell like expensive
moisturisers, now familiar. Clover's phone is under one of the
pillows. Elen picks it up. She knows the code and keys it in
without thinking: 2-5-6-8-3-7 (spelling Clover). What to do?
Actually, Elen hasn't used the internet in a long time. Weeks.
She considers looking Robert up.

Instead she searches for George. She doesn't know any of
their full names but George's. It was always the first thing that
came up when he opened his laptop, right before whatever
Channel 4 quiz show. Not a huge number of results online
for him: a couple of mentions on the Twitter account of his
university football team and some article he'd written for his
school magazine ten years ago. She finds his Facebook profile.
The wash of blue light on her face from the phone is familiar.
The scroll and swipe are easy motions to fall back into.

Does she look too cavalier, playing on a phone while
George has gone missing in a foreign country? Elen can't put

her finger on why exactly she isn't worried about him. There's something unnameable in his face and frame that just defies tragedy. He's too solid to explode. He's here, on the screen, mugging for the camera with pint froth on his nose. She looks for the rest of them on Facebook. Lyn's profile picture is from years ago; she's turning back to look at the camera, she's wearing red in some nightclub. She looks like a real teenager. Clover's is a more recent photograph of her hugging a massive black Labrador. Luka is hard to find. Luka is hard to find anywhere, in fact. She searches for his first name plus any combination of their full names. Eventually she finds him: a Luka Hansen, in the same college newsletter that announces Lyn's winning of a history prize. Elen discounts the odd buzz she feels at *that* scoop and searches, finally, for Luka Hansen.

'Incident' is a word that comes up again and again, in blue hyperlink, up and down her screen. And 'Horrific'. 'Gory.' 'Devastating.' But mainly 'Incident'. It takes Elen a moment to get her breath back, and another moment to understand that the headlines are not about Luka Hansen but his younger brother, Vince.

She finds the video. She finds it only a split second after taking a moment to appreciate how little she's been online these past few weeks. In Bend, before, her screen-time would not have been inconsiderable. There was a specific feeling of wondering what to do and then remembering that the internet existed. Here, she can fall back into the automatic gestures, scroll and swipe, with ease, but up until the point that she finds the video they seem to have relinquished their hold on her somewhat. The video, though. She comes across the link, buried on some heavy porn site and thinks about whether or not to click on it, in the way that you think about whether or not to watch porn or to start drinking, knowing that on an osteal level the decision had already been irreversibly made.

The genes are very strong. Luka's brother resembles him so closely that Elen is reminded of the first time she'd ever had to appraise Luka's face, in the Bend brewery, snow melting on the floor, him short and tanned and bright-eyed. In the video he is in someone's garden. Elen cannot tell if it is the famed English garden; it looks like it could be anywhere. He starts off close to the camera, adjusting it, talking in an Instagram patter that sounds like every other, telling us that it's a live feed. The brothers have similar voices too. Perhaps Luka's is slightly posher.

Vince moves out from the camera to reveal that there is a kid kneeling behind him. The guy looks like he's in his late teens, looks excited. There's a small pyramid of watermelons to the left of him and one watermelon on his head. It's unclear how he's balancing the watermelon so well. Possibly he has an unusually flat head, or the base of the watermelon has been somehow levelled out. Vince, eyes flashing, shows the audience that he's holding a katana. He places his hand behind the katana like an MUA background, and shows both sides of the blade. Elen would have thought that there'd be some kind of natural-disaster found-footage effect, the camera dropped, the lens shattered, the video sideways or on the fritz. But it's filmed and it's on the website, clearly and in its entirety, next to a banner for a game in which you can have cyber-sex with elves. The katana swings. The watermelon topples. The blade is stuck in the kid's head, somewhere closer to his eye than to his ear. There's blood. There's Luka – no, Vince – his face frozen. There's screaming and screaming and only after even more screaming does the camera, finally, shake and fall.

Chapter 17

Elen rolls back in the bed that isn't hers, slightly electrified. At the same time, she knows that this means nothing, except that Luka is ashamed of it. He was once adjacent to some horrible accident, so what?

It means everything. He's running away; he's creating a family.

None of the rest of the results for Vince Hansen are any more informative, although there is one article that says he got his start on YouTube as a pre-teen influencer, and there's a 2 minute and 54 second clip which is just the four seconds of mutilation footage looped to a remix of Harry Styles' 'Watermelon Sugar'. Elen turns the volume down until it's nearly mute. The track blooms tinnily over the same quick images – fruit, blade, eye, ear.

Luka calls her name and she jumps, almost blasts the video trying to pause it. She breathes in, out, and when she goes downstairs she sees Luka's found family arranged like a bizarre postcard: sat around a plate of steaming pies, the mountains blue behind them. They all look stiff. The scene reminds her of how TV murderers stage their victims in tableaux: flowers in their hair or pinned into beds like they're sleeping. She tries not thinking about TV murderers. She tries not thinking how much redder than the inside of a watermelon . . .

The kids' phones are laid out in the middle of the table on the off-chance that George calls during dinner. It must be bugging Luka, having the phones out, Elen thinks instead. They're still supposed to be getting Back To The Land!

The four of them start to eat in a strained quiet, punctuated by attempted conversation and compliments to the chef, and Elen is struggling. The peach is too hot to keep her mouth full of it and she doesn't know what to say to any of them. She makes eye contact with Lyn and is violently struck by the urge to laugh. Luka sees the suppressed laugh pass between the two of them. Elen hopes they're not in trouble. The flash of the katana; the opening above the ear; that moment when a head becomes a skull . . . No. In fact, Luka looks like he might laugh as well. Is he going to laugh?

'It is kind of funny,' he says, gesturing to George's empty seat, and she shivers. 'Like it's just funny because it's so obviously wrong. Because it's so inexcusable, if you know what I mean. Funny like where you actually can't believe that someone you've known for so long would do this.'

All quiet still. Lyn, blandly, 'It's not the best behaviour.'

As Luka's mouth gets tighter, Elen thinks of watermelon popsicles. She wonders where his conviction comes from. Why won't he give George the benefit of the doubt? She supposes the benefit of the doubt would not be to George's benefit anyway. All the places he could be if he hadn't, in fact, run off . . . Hit by a car; hurting somewhere, halfway up a mountain. *Dy-et-lov Pess.* Monsters in the hills; George face down in running water. Elen remembers his shoulders, his body moving away from her into a white mountain cloud and for the first time the sadness of his loss hits her. The need to suppress laughter has ebbed. They can't call the police, she realises. Or they could, but it would be the end of their great adventure. She thinks of Vince Hansen's katana again. Oh, she's losing it! That was a good vanishing, George had said to Luka: but now you have to bring it back.

'To be honest,' Luka is saying, 'I don't know what I would do if he came back.' (Elen looks to see if the 'if' is killing Clover, but her face is perfectly neutral.) 'Would we let him come to Turkey? It's hard because it's just an immaculately planned journey. Planned with care. Planned with fucking love.' Luka is spitting by the end of this last sentence, and then very abruptly he starts to look like he'll laugh again. 'It's like someone dipping on a highly calibrated bank heist, you know. It's disrespectful. It endangers us. And also,' he pushes the plate away, 'It's not new. He does this on every night out.'

Elen's father is an easy-going man. He had expected to understand his child more, and when he found that he didn't really get Elen he had been happy to let her grow up and away from him, but he is fundamentally an affable guy. This meant that when Elen began to encounter angry men it took her a while to realise what she was seeing. A lot of women are first inured to the angry-man tirade by their fathers. For Elen, it was a few of her teachers, then a couple of her friends' boyfriends, and then Robert (but only occasionally and for a little while).

Men often express anger in long, performative monologues. These monologues are intended to soothe the speaker and to frighten the listener. There are often physical accompaniments – doors slammed, walls punched, veins a-throb. Robert had monologued a couple of times before Elen got fed up of it. After that, she would so thoroughly investigate the first sign of any slight or complaint from him that it was impossible for him to take it any further. Their last few years together had been a tirade-free stalemate, and though cruel words were said often, they were said quietly.

It was weird and pitiful to watch Luka spit and flush and clench his fists, like watching animal young do a stumbling version of the thing that was most in their nature. George was right though: the group means everything to Luka. While it's in place, his loyalty is cheerful, twinkly, absolute. As soon as it comes apart, something alarmed and angry takes that loyalty's place.

Luka is still going on about how George does this 'every night out in London. He gets too drunk and he Irish goodbyes. I mean, he's a fucking baby. Really, it's I'm A Drunk Sixth Former stuff.' His rage seems to be accelerating. He's smacking his lips quite a bit.

The Irish goodbye theory rings a shameful bell somewhere in Elen's lower gut. There had been a period, back in Michigan and just out of school, when Elen had been less adjusted to drinking, which was not to say drinking less. Elen had been a runner back then: she would hit a point every so often, a certain level of drunkenness, and just peel off into the night. Friends, Liberty, would make a shot at chasing her.

The next day she'd have to explain that she wasn't looking for attention or trying to make anyone follow her. She was just a runner. Still is.

Lyn's phone hums from the middle of the table. She's minimised the notification before anyone can read it but not before Elen's reminded of Lyn ignoring her mother's calls. Going ghost and Irish goodbyes are of a kind, she thinks; you only need to decide that you will no longer be beholden. Luka's really found his groove. His reedy voice accelerates. 'George runs off all the time.' He looks at Clover, who is still visibly distressed. 'Listen,' he says with great gravity. 'I've been through his stuff. He took his passport.'

Lyn's face doesn't change at this revelation. Elen hopes hers does, if only out of sympathy with Clover, who cannot stop herself from saying, 'But he left his tobacco!'

'Clover. He took his *passport*.' He transfers his gaze to Elen, appealingly. 'Look, this isn't when your girlfriend goes missing after a night out, okay, or after going home late by herself. This is when your dad goes to the shop for cigarettes and doesn't come back.' His eyes stay on Elen as though he's thinking and then he drops them suddenly. 'I mean. Not *your* dad, necessarily.'

'My dad's okay,' she says, bemused.

Luka changes direction. 'To be honest, it's usually because of a girl. Anything cunty he does is usually because of a girl.'

Lyn raises her eyebrows.

'Anything he does at all, really. I mean the whole reason he agreed to come skiing was because of the crystal-shop girl. Perhaps he's run off back to her.' His sentences are taking on a supervillain cadence. He's no longer out of control; these are careful words, designed to provoke. 'Maybe he's running from a girl in Banff, who knows?'

'Okay, enough. I'll admit it,' says Elen. 'It was me.' The joke is partly to undermine Luka, partly just to stem his attack. He laughs, takes another peach turnover and tears it open.

'You're a real ski-fox, Elen. I'm sorry to be so grumpy. It's just the way he is, it bugs me. He falls in and out of love, like, professionally.' Then he looks at Clover, who is brimming with tears.

'Luka, I wanted to tell you.'

'Tell me what, Clovey? Hey now, don't cry.'

'We were. We were sleeping together.'

It all comes out in a soft gulping flood. She is not a pretty crier. She admits it all: the loving, the love, the hiding it. The most surprising part is Lyn's unfeigned shock. Elen realises that a part of her always assumed that Lyn has always known all of it. Her composure is usually unshakeable, which has translated into an aura of cool omniscience. But she's agape now, even as Luka stays tightly smiling; she's shaken and fascinated by this thing that's been hiding in her house for months. George and Clover's on-again-off-again holding of each other unfolds at length over the table that is none of theirs. George himself is miles away in whichever direction. Elen pictures him hiking against the wind, uphill and into a snowstorm, but it might be that he's just at a bar. George and Robert and whichever family it was that originally sat around this table in this corner of Banff pressing glitter glue into the wood: all are anywhere, everywhere, exploded.

*

From somewhere behind Clover comes the sound of a small pearl. The sound, the pearl, drops from the faucet into the sink; a little plash, pealing underneath the noise of her crying. Another pearl drops. Then another, faster, then the necklace breaks. When Elen looks past George's empty seat she sees that blood is running out of the tap. Red blood.

It's blood without a doubt; she knows what rust in the pipes looks like and this stuff is opaque, thick, filling up the sink. She doesn't say anything. The basin starts to overflow, though the tap lever is all the way down, pushed to closed. The way that she can see the blood is different from how she could see George hiking into a snowstorm or her exploded husband or even the remembered katana undoing someone's skull. This isn't in her head. Blood is pouring out onto the counter and soon will hit the floor and she is watching it with real open eyes. She doesn't say anything, she tries to unpicture it. Only when Lyn goes to fill up her water glass does the blood disappear.

Chapter 18

+++

After the dust has settled in everyone's throats, Luka takes a walk. Some time to think. There's nothing to gain from being objectionable, and everything to lose, a whole utopia in the balance, so he doesn't draw attention to his going out and soon he's disappeared into the trees that surround the house.

He walks fast, observes the green feathery heights of the trees. They go on densely, for further than he remembers. He walks in loops, making the ring of fir trees into a forest, or a country. Minutes in, a thick shiver rolls over his shoulders. Of course he's forgotten his scarf. He scuffs one foot against the other, wondering if it would undermine him to go back for it, and then walks faster: pulls the neck of the jacket over his mouth, huffs into it for warmth. The cold has his eyes stinging. Keeping secrets is poisonously anti-social. Luka gives his friends everything and in return they hold back.

Something comes speeding past him, skips to a twitching stop a few metres away, a rabbit. A hare? It assumes that motherly pose, upright on its haunches, ears cocked, paws drawn neatly to its breast. The snow is in thin patches.

One of Vince's earliest videos, made when he was about ten, had involved pranking a school friend into believing that he had cooked her pet rabbit. It wasn't an elegant deception; it was really just a lie, with some ketchup splatters in the microwave as supporting evidence. The internet loved it regardless.

Luka had been tasked with hiding in the living room, holding the real rabbit on his lap, out of sight. He'd wanted to expose the trick, to help the crying girl in the kitchen, but his father told him sternly not to spoil his brother's games.

Besides, there was a sinister gravity to Vince, an authority that belied his age. If Luka wasn't helping, he was the one being pranked. He can feel the prickle of it now – the sudden understanding of having been deceived. It was the stamp of his childhood. The videos started getting serious views a couple of years after the rabbit trick, and all his accumulating successes – first thousand followers, first ten thousand, first million views – were reported at the breakfast table. At first, Luka had been earnestly happy at each milestone, even proud. Less so when he was fifteen and Vince was twelve with a career and serious money and now stacked enough to trip up his big brother every time he passed. Less so when he was seventeen and Vince was putting out videos every day, pranks and internet challenges; being paid for club appearances; filling juice bottles with worms and filming Luka taking a swig.

'Action inspires further action,' their father had said of the juice-bottle incident. Mr Hansen was evangelical about the superiority of deeds to words, which, in combination with a bluff respect for money-making, made him as proud of

Vince's videos as it made him unappreciative of Luka's Model UN passions. Hot air, he said to that. He liked impressing upon his family the importance of 'doing it for themselves', their father. Luka still can't say what 'it' is.

One summer a pigeon had died. This wouldn't normally scratch the surface of Luka's father's consciousness, except that the pigeon had been roosting under a railway bridge some minutes from their house and the corpse had fallen a foot, got caught up in barbed wire and been left suspended by one red leg, wings out in a kind of Christ pose. It was still there weeks later. Luka got into the habit of crossing the street when he had to walk under the railway bridge. Neither weather, nor birds, nor the train overhead had any power to dislodge it. His mother found it upsetting and so his father placed a complaint with the local council. Two months passed without response, Luka's dad muttering about inaction with increasing ire. The pigeon corpse had not decayed at all. After three months it was fresh as the day of death; it had not been pecked or even weathered. It's a security camera, Vince had insisted, disguised as decussate dead bird. In the end, their father shot the corpse down himself. Not being a camera, it burst into fifty fleshy pieces. ('If you want something done,' their father had said, satisfied by both the shot and the lesson taught.)

Luka hadn't understood the value of the lesson until after he'd left for university. He'd always felt protective, deeply, of any underdog; he still does. *As* an underdog, he directed towards himself the same love that he felt for the hosts of traumatised rabbits. At thirteen he kissed his own skinned knees. Today the trees rustle round Hanneke and he blows

warm air quite tenderly into his jacket. He used to write in
to news shows when he felt they'd sided unfairly with power:
impassioned letters, invocating justice. Hot air, his dad said
to that as well. But at university, finding himself 'bludgeoned
by the burgeoning vogue for identity politics', words began
to lose their charm. (Although he *was* pleased to have struck
upon the bludgeon/burgeon thing.) No action was taken
at all. Student activism was no different from high school
debate: it was only the competitive manipulation of words.
'We need to shoot this dead bird,' he thought, but that didn't
translate. His university flatmate was 'cancelled' for blasting
spirituals, songs of freedom from the underground railroad,
after breaking up with her boyfriend. And for tweeting 'Free
At Last, Free At Last'. Luka, partly emboldened by a vague
idea that she might now sleep with him, was outraged on
her behalf.

How little Oxford had lived up to his expectations. The
spires did not hold his attention; the historic stone was cold.
His college hadn't even got round to putting heating in all
the rooms. It was the opposite of freedom, of course; it was
the bonds of civilisation dressed up and raised to the power
of ten. And even from his college room, he could see that
the bonds did not fall away once you left the place. They
followed you all your life. (Look at Clover, who knew every
third person at her circle-jerk computer firm. How hard it is
to find the untracked path.) It was even worse at Oxford's
masonic lodge, though they said appealing things about blood
oaths and Oscar Wilde. It was quite difficult to watch. Hoods
and blindfolds, when anyone could find the exact text of a
Swearing In ritual on the first page of Google. And all over,

the bonds of ordinariness and civilisation wound once, twice, three times round. There was his seminar tutor; there was the student association president; there was his other seminar tutor, pretending not to recognise the first. None of these people could live up to the distinction of their regalia. But a man had given him a book.

Luka read it that same evening in his college library, and something did change. The lilac crept over the alcoves; a clever man from Michigan was falling asleep over his demotic French at the table behind. Luka stayed up, kept reading in the room's tall dim. He felt he was doing something quite important.

He'd not been having much success with women that winter, which isn't relevant but which sets the scene. It was cold, he was at a loose end. The pink tome flared with invocations of sexual freedom, utopia, action. Action most of all. Luka went on a date with a woman who could not stop sneezing; he imagined holding a pillow over her face while he fucked her and was then appalled at himself; Vince's fake phone calls and creative use of saran wrap, meanwhile, had all the blonde doyennes of Instagram in his videos and on his arm. Luka wasn't jealous; reading Fourier, he understood that in fact he was stifled.

And then Vince had killed that boy.

Their father accused Luka of being glad when it happened. 'You were always waiting for Vinny to slip up,' he'd said. But Luka hadn't been glad at all. In fact, he'd had nightmares for months, awful nightmares, real fear. Vince had always possessed this unspeakable power, the power of prodigy, of showing Luka up; a power that correlated to the taste of worms in the morning. Now Luka knew that the power existed outside of his own imagination. And when Vince got away with it (550k in restitution to the family, suspended sentence) his older brother knew that he was through with what Fourier called civilisation, knew that he had to find another family.

+++

It's dark. The ragged patches of white on the ground are indistinguishable from everything else except for the sound as Luka puts his feet down, a squeaking or a muffled sound depending on the thickness. They're good, walks. He should walk more often.

Yesterday on the mountain, he'd described to George his vision of utopia. Buzzing on acid, loving his friends, ears full of the skid and rattle of hard snow. The girls were some way behind, around some white corner; he'd spoken to George privately because he wanted to tell George first! Oh, the phalanstery had lived when he talked about it. *It will be started somewhere rural, remote; it will be home to pleasures that are not Spartan ... Diversity of region and people is the most important thing: valley, stream, forest, mountain; a thousand people in a state of what Fourier called 'graduated inequality, as to wealth, age, personality, and knowledge.'* Yesterday when Luka'd pictured it, the phalanstery had spires better than Oxford's and a covered courtyard like at school. (George had laughed at this.)

Luka's on his fourth circuit. He ought to have gone into town, he thinks. He'd been nearly ready to cry at the start of the walk; he isn't now. There's wind in his eyes, plus his walking has been vigorous and warmed him quite thoroughly. See: action inspires further action. George had laughed and had left, but Luka has more than nothing. Clover's a good girl. She's still there, even if she had lied. Luka won't tell her off any more, he decides; he'd done well to reel it in at dinner, retreat into *I'm not angry, of course I'm not angry. I'm disappointed that you would think that I was angry.* He still has his commander-in-chief. Elen's still with them. Luka will keep them all safe; he'll establish their harbour.

Something makes noise at his side but he can't see anything. Perhaps it's the rabbit, thinks Luka. He smiles at the thought that he's letting it live.

+++

Chapter 19

Elen's going to think about the blood later. Luka's going down the route of *I'm not angry, of course I'm not angry. I'm disappointed that you would think that I was angry* and Elen's going to think about the blood later. The kitchen is full of palpable discomfort. Clover's eyes are swollen; she looks chastened but also like she would quite like to go to sleep. Both retire to their rooms. The house is then heavy with the stillness that comes from being closed off by the mountains.

Elen gets up and goes to the sink. 'Why does he care so much?' she asks Lyn, turning on the tap which runs obediently: high pressure, crystal clear. (Not blood. It's such a well-appointed home.)

In spite of the fact that this kitchen opens straight on to the sitting room with its couch and its kilim, it has successfully assumed the legacy of traditional kitchens, separated from the living rooms by a door: somewhere for women to talk. It feels suddenly, excitingly collusive. They keep their voices lowered. When she looks round she sees that it's taking a second for all of Lyn's features to start working together again: she's still occupied by the surprise of it all, by the subterfuge.

'He doesn't like things being hidden from him,' Lyn begins. She speaks neutrally, with a kind of relish. As she continues, it becomes clear that even with the rising kitchen closeness, in this home of orange juice and wine, she will not be indiscriminate or overly revealing. She will stand by Luka. 'George disappearing was a dick move. That's pretty undeniable. So he's hurt that that was hidden, and he's worried about the group disintegrating. But mostly, I think, he puts a lot of effort into this, into Turkey and the whole communal thing, and he's sort of envisioning it falling apart. Though it oughtn't necessarily.'

Elen bunts her toe against the sideboard. The strip of metal between carpet and tile is coming up. It's caught them all out at different times. ('I'm glad we're not paying to stay here,' George had said; 'I'd sue.' But Elen had wondered if it was the work of the glitter-glue child: the absent family re-asserting their presence.) When she asks Lyn if she's sure that George isn't in trouble, that he's simply left of his own accord, Lyn nods, definite and serene. It's nearly reassuring this time, that coolness of hers. At least, it is until Elen pictures how she'd react if it was Elen that disappeared. The response she envisages is something akin to a stone being dropped into a huge blue-green lake. Small ripples, lasting up to a minute. A girl who ghosts her own mother can walk away from anyone. Elen smiles.

'So you really back him?' she asks. 'You don't think this is crazy? Or juvenile.'

'Well it's a bit nuts to go after Clover. She's a teddy bear. It's not juvenile though, for him. Look, okay, it's like a horseshoe. When you're kids, friendship is the most important thing, right, it's apex, it's everything. If someone doesn't play with you at lunch it's significant and cruel. Then you grow up and out of it. You don't really owe people your time, or much more than civility. If someone doesn't see you for a few weeks, you can't hold it against them. But for Luka it's horseshoed, he's grown back into it. Friendship is everything again. It's total love, total commitment.'

'Hm. Should I feel bad that he hasn't asked me to be his blood brother yet?' Total love at last, total commitment at last? What a turn of events. The tap is running still, resolutely water. At last Elen turns it off. Perhaps what she'd seen had been the result of old acid. She lets out her breath, and the smell of peaches and burnt brown sugar rises around them.

'Oh, you're getting there,' Lyn says. 'He thinks you're delightful.'

At some point in the evening Luka goes for a walk. After the door has closed a chill and the smell of vinegar go through the front room. Lyn seems to think that a walk will calm him down, though Clover points out that he hasn't taken his scarf; all three of them can sense an anger that he has not yet properly articulated. There's a restlessness left behind him. At a loose end once again Elen goes exploring, which is to say: she snoops. It's not that the watermelon-gore video has put her in the mood; if anything it's the ghosts of the family that once lived here. She had started to see everywhere the traces of their eradicated community. Glitter, like bones. But mostly, it was the feeling reaffirmed that she was living among a bewildering people.

George has left little relics all over the boys' room – slippers, boxers rucked up at the end of the bed, his copy of *The Silmarillion*. A gleam of cologne in a blue travel bottle. Elen tucks this last away into a dresser drawer lest Clover uncork it and become overcome with yearning. The last thing they need is the melodrama that arises in the wake of being left in the night, and she knows it too well.

George had only left that day, or perhaps that night. Robert had been missing for two months. Still, there are familiar patterns of behaviour that she can identify in Clover. Checking her phone. Checking Facebook. Looking in the mirror, as though there might be some clue in the lines of her face. As though he might have left because of how she'd had her hair that day. They were different leavings, George and Robert's, different vanishings in the night, but the rejection was of the same family. When Robert had left Elen she was hurt in a way that she hadn't experienced for decades, a way she hadn't imagined she was still capable of. Marriage was supposed to be the end of that feeling, of the feeling of being left. The idea goes that until marriage, you're never truly secure. And although their relationship had been, on more than one level, long dead, it had stunned Elen that she had been bad enough, mean enough, rude, ugly, cold enough (the words rotated in her head, and were always said in her own voice) that he'd actually left. Actually-leaving is hard. It returned under the lens a whole kaleidoscope of rejections: school canteen missteps; the new girlfriend of the woman she thought would never get over her; even the thing you can feel over the phone to someone where you know they love you less. Clover had it now. She had the warmth lurched away from her, had the hand slip from around her waist and the body roll out of her bed.

Elen closes the drawer, pauses, re-opens it. There's something pink and trashy in the corner where she's stashed the cologne. It is, of course, *The Utopian Vision of Charles Fourier: Selected Texts on Work, Love and Passionate Attraction*. A huge pencil drawing of an eye takes up most of the front cover. It looks out of place on the cover of a book about the eighteenth century, like a kid's drawing. Elen gets into George's bed, which smells of smoke and sweat. She leaves the covers off, holds Fourier down by her lap and opens it.

Luka is all over the book. It's marked up, underscored and annotated in different inks the way that the maps were. For every line she reads, his asides pronounce themselves in that familiar, reedy, excitable voice. Elen's not reading this thing cover to cover – she follows the tideline of Luka's notes, which start with a massive vortical circling of one sentence.

Sometimes radicalisation is just what happens when you stop identifying as an individual and start identifying as part of a collective. Luka's writing overlaps sometimes. It peeps through the gaps between sentences. Elen reads in triplicate, hearing her own voice, Luka's, and the dead man's. The passages that seem to interest him the most are the ones concerning group psychology. Fourier has elaborate taxonomies of social groups, none of which include the word friendship. He identifies False Groups, Simple Groups, Compound Groups, Bastard Compound Groups and Pure Compound Groups. '*The term "group" is conventionally applied to any sort of gathering, even to a band of idlers who come together out of boredom with no passion or purpose – even to an assemblage of empty-minded individuals who are busy killing time and waiting for something to happen.'* Luka highlights this in pink, with a HAHA.

The highlighting becomes more frequent and less obviously tongue-in-cheek when Fourier starts to break down how exactly to form a balanced group that could become a perfect phalanx. Elen reads about the well-structured group for about three minutes before she gets bored. Fourier says the same thing in a hundred different ways: a balanced group dynamic is not only optimal but part of the natural order – like planets, or a perfect garden. The next tracts cover his 'proto-feminism' (Luka's words). Fourier veers wildly from contempt to reverence for women; the marginalia seem to follow his lead.

'To attempt to judge women by the character that they display in Civilization is like [. . .] judging beavers by the sluggishness that they show in captivity,' . . . *'Woman in a state of liberty will surpass man in all the mental and bodily functions which are not related to physical strength.'* . . . *'Women exist in financial slavery to men.'*

She reads over the passage relating to this last line more thoroughly, then reads it again. The thinking slides momentarily into place; it feels real and applicable. It was Elen who had never been at liberty, Elen who was still in financial slavery. Robert had been unhappy, but his hand had always been on the tiller. When he left he had taken her home with him. She had been sluggish – drunk and depressed – in a captivity designed by men, never financially independent, packaging other people's quail eggs. Her eye skips down the page, delighted, horrified, bypassing Luka's heavy hand for a second. The dead author comes to life, starts whispering in

Elen's ear, extolling a Harmony where she had never had to wash Robert's greasy dishes. Then he writes something like *'In the barbarian order it is necessary to brutalize women, [. . .] in the civilized order it is necessary to stupefy women from their childhood'* and she's back to remembering that he is, in fact, a five-moons crazy.

Luka identifies only one important sentence in the 'Marriage and the family system' chapter: *'The institution of marriage fosters universal deception and sexual dishonesty.'* After that, his annotations begin to converge on a theme.

'Taste for variety in sexual partners is natural', he's underlined, with a slightly kitschy exclamation mark. *'Sexual relations fuel social change.'* By the line *'The laws protect debauchery when it is practiced by genteel ladies [. . .] by young ladies who have a taste for pleasure'* he's written 'Emma!' Poor Emma, she thinks.

Fourier predicted a *'new social order based on the liberation and utilization of erotic energies ignored / misused / misdirected.'* Luka has underscored this quite furiously. Elen chuckles. She thinks of that big drinking night when they had celebrated her first decision to stay longer with the group, the highly sexed energies that she'd imagined moving like beams of light between the kids. If Luka was to stoke those normal post-adolescent feelings, already intensified by alcohol, he would have some real power. He could give the group a magnetic sticking-power, like the air around a nightclub. George and Clover have been 'misdirecting' these energies, she supposes.

'Sexual perversions are the last test of Fourierian ethics, with his refusal to see wrong in any passion. Sexual fantasies must be satisfied, lest anything be left to chance.' Luka has written this part, of course. It slopes excitedly off the page. Sexual fantasies *must* be satisfied ... Perhaps if she quotes Luka back to himself he'll go a little easier on Clover.

There are pages and pages on pleasure. Fourier's was apparently hedonistic in comparison to the other, more restrained utopias of the nineteenth century.

'Sensual pleasure is the only weapon that God can use to master us.' ... *'Good food is only one-half of gastronomic pleasure: [...] The most affluent and refined civilized gentleman cannot, even at his country house, bring together as well-matched and varied a selection of guests as the poorest man of Harmony will find at all his meals.'*

A well-matched and varied selection of guests, Elen thinks, that's me. I'm the selection. It's a version of a thought she's had before, when Luka was talking about hash and his 'authentic Bend inhabitant': that he had plucked her from that brewery to serve up to his little friends. And doesn't Luka use pleasure to keep all the group in their place, like Fourier's God? Doesn't he use food, weed, affirmation, adrenaline to manacle the group together and doesn't he believe that (having originated and curated these pleasures for his friends) they owe him a level of obedience? But there's nothing so terrible about that: it's not unusual to expect a degree of gratitude and natural social reciprocity, though Elen herself is out of the habit of both. The peculiarities begin to accumulate in the next chapter.

Fourier is pro-pleasure; Luka even uses the word hedonism in his marginalia. But it becomes apparent that in his utopia, sexual variance is regulated. Psychotically regulated.

'In Harmony social relations are organized in such a way that

no amorous intrigue can remain unknown.' The chapter starts
softly. Elen is wry at this one. *'Three or four years of fidelity
may be too much to ask of a human being.'* She is wry at this
one too, and thinks of the girl at Robert's bank. What a world
away that girl was now, in her thin shirt, and had she ever
been on an adventure like Elen's?

Fourier theorises different sexual combinations: people
entwined every which way. Girl, boy, girl; two partners and
a friend; six different lovers rotating hexagonally around an
emotionally committed, sexually polygamous duo. The con-
figurations begin to test Elen, mathematically rather than
morally. He suggests *'a polygamous form of love in which a man
or woman has concurrent physical relationships with two partners. Each partner consents to the pleasures of the other, and the
friendship among all three is redoubled as a result of this bond.
[. . .] Such relationships will also rely in part on the activation
of homosexual love, that ambiguous form of love which our cus-
toms do not tolerate even though it was accepted in antiquity.'*
He's deeply and anachronistically sympathetic to lesbians
and believes children under fifteen should be kept clear of all
information on sexual matters. This appeals to Elen on one
level although, for whatever reason, thinking of Luka deciding to be sympathetic to lesbians makes her feel slightly sick.
(She imagines him nodding feelingly as Lyn tells him about
her ex-girlfriend, the one at the lake.)

Once of age, citizens of the utopia are divided into damsels and vestals, i.e. sex-havers and virgins. They form two
flanks, the damselate and the vestalate. *'Children will revere
the vestals and disdain the damsels,'* Fourier writes, although,
he emphasises, both are necessary to the survival of the

community. *'The vestals will become the idols of the whole phalanx [. . .] the handsomest male vestal will greet the princess at the gate.'* There's a threshold that piques Elen's interest – being seventeen and deciding whether to identify as a slut or a maid. *'All of the young tribes regard the vestals with the sort of affection that one feels toward a group which has remained faithful after a schism.'*

It's fully dark outside now. Luka will be home soon, surely. Unless he's following suit and has taken off in the night after George, leaving all the womenfolk behind. Like in wartime. Elen thinks she wouldn't mind that. The pines rattle outside in the sour dark and she thinks about schisms. Maybe it reflects well on Luka that his claim to socialism is founded on being totally mad rather than simply out of touch.

Assuming he comes home, it'll be soon anyway, and she doesn't want to him to catch her – not that she's doing anything wrong. She sets the covers right, puts the room back to how she found it, sits on top of the bed and starts to skim through the next chapter.

Fourier foresees couples so angelic that they love each other purely platonically. Angelic does not equate to totally sexless, however; *'Angelic couples preserve their chastity by establishing a network of carnal relations with other people of both sexes.*

'Almost every town and village has at least one extraordinarily handsome man and one extraordinarily beautiful woman. These individuals excite everyone's desires and passions. Narcisse and Psyche are the most beautiful people in the town of Cnidos; everyone adores them and one could cite at least twenty Cnidian men

who have an avowed passion for Psyche and twenty Cnidian women who are burning with the same desire for Narcisse.'

Elen reads this two or three times, wondering why Luka has starred it so heavily in the margins and how these villagers got so unlucky as to be named Psyche and Narcisse, before she conceives that he, Luka, might be identifying with the extraordinarily handsome man. She doesn't need a minute to figure out who might be Psyche. Long walks in the field some way outside of college and not a single sexual spark between them? 'A romance in a way.' Naturally.

Chapter 20

They go to bed still full of peach. It feels like making a concession to a child, like a whole family having breakfast for dinner.
Elen's happy not to be sharing a room. She looks through the
water bottle for the little ghost.

It's early enough when she gets up that Elen expects to have
the kitchen to herself so that she can have a coffee and think
some things through. But when she goes downstairs Clover
is there, making porridge on the hob, browning apple slices
in maple syrup for it. Part of Elen wants to go to her and
say sorry, sorry for not being more helpful when Luka was
channelling bad energy at you. But that's kids' talk; however
softly Clover wishes her a good morning, Elen is not about to
identify something as bad energy, and he hadn't really done
more than that. She asks Clover how she's doing though and
(in the spirit of overture) says she thought that she, Elen,
might cook the group's dinner today. Clover cries.

The cry translates completely to the face but is entirely
silent. There are the tears, the flush, the operatic mouth;
there is no sob. It's frighteningly obvious that she is used to
the hard and quiet cry. Naturally the thing of needing not to

make noise accelerates the upset: the whole injustice of it all amplifies and flares up on Clover's face and then it is gone. She leans back against the stove and wipes her eyes. Had it been unbearably romantic, Elen wanted to know, their subterfuge among the slopes?

'Do you think it's weird,' she says instead. 'The way no one is worried about him?' It is Lyn's serenity she's thinking of, and the insistence, the devotion, to the idea that nothing could possibly have happened. The Lotus Eaters, back at it again.

Clover looks troubled, but she says, 'He took his *passport*,' in Luka's voice.

Elen nods. She pushes away the image of Luka cutting up the passport with the big silver sewing scissors that had been used to divide the acid.

'Are you missing him?'

'I'm fuming, to be honest,' says Clover. 'I'm really fuming. No one saw – no one, literally in the world, knew exactly what went on between us, so no one knows how entirely fucked up it is that he's left like this.'

Elen gets up from the table to put her hand briefly on Clover's forearm; the gesture is awkward but sweet. Clover breaks the story down, and although it starts in Argentina and follows plate lines across to the European glaciers, it's not totally unfamiliar.

The whole thing had started as a casual, drunken one off. They hadn't even slept together the first time, though of course they did a few days later. 'Interior: Yurt – and so on,' until he was kissing her under the nearest pine tree, Lyn and

Luka waiting for them at the bottom of a pink mountain, and Clover was saying, 'This doesn't feel casual to me any more'. There was a panic at this point because they had been keeping it from the others, feeling instinctively that Luka would see it as something trouble-making.

'So, George decided that we should leave it there. And we did, for about a week, until Luka thought he saw something – a touch under the table, whatever – and dragged George off to interrogate him. And then George came to me and was like, oh my god, Luka was saying this and this and I think he's on to us, I think I deflected him, and we were just laughing because it was so ridiculous and then we, you know.'

'Fell back into each other's arms,' Elen offers.

'Exactly. But the whole thing was crazy. Conducting – anything – in secret when you are living in two tents, or one yurt, or one empty Airbnb? It's like two people trying to have secret sex in a square room containing four people. It's like . . . It's like *Huis Clos*. And I thought it meant something, that we managed it. We were communicating in secret looks. We had a whole language.'

The feelings grew, of course. He got travelsick in Hintertux and she looked after him, of course. They went white water rafting in Bend. Everything he wanted to do delighted her. They spent an afternoon in the abandoned resort just kissing in the room with the broken lock that had been full of dust and skis. George had bared his teeth; Clover had closed her eyes; rabbits and moons and clowns with Elizabethan ruffs had spun all across the ceiling. 'He said things that weren't, you know. Commitments. But that were kernels of commitment. Or presaged commitment.'

'Like what?'

'Like I want to live in your belly button.'

'Oh.'

'But do you know what I mean? How totally confusing it is to have him say that to me, and all these other intense little kernels of affirmation, and for us to maintain on the outside that we're not really any closer than he is to Lyn or I am to Luka?' continues Clover. She wants to say: his hand found mine in odd moments. Instead she says, 'But in practice it was easy. Especially since given the chance Lyn and Luka would split off into their—'

'Angelic couple?'

'Yeah, I guess. They've always been faster skiers as well.'

'Luka finding out was just never an option. I hate him being mad at me, and you can tell he is. He just is really, really, like . . . ' She searches for the word. 'Anti-cronyism.'

'I don't know about cronyism. You're just kids in love.' She considers offering for discussion some of the things that she'd read in Luka's handwriting the night before. She wonders if Clover could shed some light on whatever strange teen-Brit irony she'd missed. No – it's clear that a joint deconstruction of Luka's copy of *The Utopian Vision of Charles Fourier* is not the kind of healing Clover wants right now, even if everything she says confirms the slight weirdness at which those notes had hinted.

'In the house in Italy he used to sit between us on the sofa. He joked about George and me being couple-y and we had no idea if he knew or not; because, I mean, Luka would sort of flirt with me as well, as a joke. And George encouraged it, he even laughed to throw off suspicion. When I told George

I couldn't bear it – not the flirting but him laughing at it – he kissed me all over and said, "Haven't you guessed?" He would send it in secret notes which I would destroy. He would write it in snow for me. When we were in the same aisle of the supermarket and everyone else was in a different section . . . oho.' Clover looks wistful. When Luka walks in, she puts the porridge in a bowl for him.

The skiing that day is perfect, which is bizarre. Frightening, even: how quickly everything reforms to fill the space that someone leaves behind. It feels odd that George isn't in the car and there's a marked difference between waiting for four people to catch up with you at the end of a descent and waiting for three, but everything just goes right. Elen's on perfect form – sharp turns, smooth climbs, immaculate slalom through the landforms. Everything clicks, and they can all feel it; even Clover is turning every ridge into a jump. She looks like an advert. For the first time since getting to Banff, Elen thinks of what might come after. They will say goodbye to the slope. She will go to Turkey, unless she goes to Michigan. She might ski for a year. She might get a job. Perhaps the world will end.

The man with blue eyes appears in AT skis, as suddenly as in a vision. He's traversed the valley already this morning, starting at Lake Minnewanka. It's all downhill from here, he tells her, and winks before he leaves. Luka looks over with interest at Elen and her apparent friend. Lyn might be smiling. There's a real gap waiting after Banff and it could turn into just about anything. Elen remembers how when she was first considering getting married to Robert she'd thought that she had plumped for an easier life by picking a boy.

After she swings instinctively to look in the direction of Lake Minnewanka some five miles away and hidden by hillside, it comes to her that the skiing is perfect because today she properly knows the mountain. This is more of a feat when the skiing is backcountry and the parts she's working with have not been anatomised, levelled, labelled. Perhaps Luka has a crazy map of this side of the mountain hidden somewhere, with each contour immortalised, but what Elen knows is that for days it seemed totally disparate and by the tenth hike and tenth descent it has all suddenly come together in her head. She might kiss the ground. She might tip her hat to Mount Bachelor, back in Bend, Oregon. Once she had just been a girl who wanted to live in a mountain town because she liked mountains.

When they get back to Hanneke, Elen feels like her palate has been cleansed. She's the last one in; she closes the door behind her, and the cold air that has been circulating her nose and throat is gradually saturated by the smell of the Airbnb. It smells like cooking and laundry and the people she knows. It fells her with its familiarity.

Between this sense of homecoming and the happy exhaustion of having skied so well, she's hard to annoy. Luka is radiating an eagerness to make amends. He jokes, he heads straight to the dishes, he twists Clover's ponytail round his index finger. It feels like it could over-compensate for George's absence but she knows that it's mainly because he's understood how embarrassing his fury was yesterday. Good for him. The try-hardness reminds her a little of Robert in the early days, back when he still shocked at how hard it could be to get on with a person, but Luka wears it better.

Luka, of course, cooks dinner. Elen chops garlic. She's introspective and comfortable, insulated from his chatter.

'Clover seemed way better today, right?' he says. She nods and he continues, topping up her glass, 'I think George thought she would miss him for longer.'

'What?'

'Like, I bet George thought she would miss him for longer.'

'George thought she would miss him for longer? Did he say that to you? Did he tell you he was leaving?'

'Elen, imagine. As if I would have let him leave. Surely it's just such an easy guess. It's George.'

The 'surely' is easily delivered and disproportionately convincing, although Elen's calmness has evaporated.

'Sure,' she says. 'It's George.'

She wonders at Luka's keenness as he fills their plates and talks too much. Assuming he's not covering anything up, he's madly overcompensating for the day before. Had she perhaps made a mistake in the Bend brewery all that time ago – are these teenagers perhaps not cool and in fact only rich? Cool is measured on such a different meter these days, and the conversion's hard with them being British. It's not like it was twenty-five years ago when she was hustling *Playboy* from older boys in the canteen. Luka's touchy with Clover throughout dinner, playing with her hair, holding her pinkies. It looks sort of like a boy trying to make up with his mother, but the sex-obsessed marginalia in the Fourier have her feeling itchy. *Taste for variety in sexual partners is natural. Young ladies who have a taste for pleasure. Sexual fantasies must be satisfied, lest anything be left to chance.*

*

Unease and dinner (pasta, heavy on the Philadelphia) leave her warm and distracted. Her thoughts are uneven, discontinuous: she does one lap of the house looking for her goggles and then another, declining offers of help.

The laps take a long time for such a small house. Odd recesses reveal themselves to her, and new bays in the walls; high shelves she's never spotted, which hold shadows. Elen finds herself suddenly apprehensive about pulling back the shower curtain, like a kid, and a thin cupboard in a corner at the end of the corridor upstairs summons that feeling she'd had in the haunted resort when she had first considered all the dark locked rooms that shared walls with the places they ate and slept. Ridiculous, obviously. Hanneke isn't abandoned and cannot frighten; she's a lit-up family home, outfitted for guests, designed to welcome ... But the cupboard sings in a thin high pitch of something about to come out of it. She has seen this cupboard before. It was where Lyn put her skis when that car had pulled up and they'd all thought they'd been found out and that the Mounties would be round any second. She had hidden them like a body, Elen had thought at the time.

A terrible, terrible understanding presents itself. If she opens this cupboard, it will be George that falls out. This is where Luka has put him. Clover will miss me, he'll have promised, and Luka will have laughed. '*Ills must all be denounced; half-hearted criticism only serves to worsen the evil.*' She puts her hand to the latch. What would a dead boy's freckles look like? The cupboard holds its quavering note. Whatever shadowy thing is inside it calls to her – and Elen pulls the latch – and the call heightens, thins – and the door moves open of its own accord – and inside are only various Hoover attachments and a basket filled with bright plastic clothespins.

'Fuck,' she says (too loud) and then, under her breath, 'Idiot, idiot, idiot.' She spins on her heel into the bright hallway and puts a hand on the back of her head like she's checking it's still there. Then she knocks on her own door and layers up.

Stood outside the house, Elen lets her breathing slow and looks about at the tall trees that surround Hanneke, considering the direction in which she should begin walking.

'Hello.' Lyn appears at the door. 'You disappearing off to hook up with George?'

Elen exhales, laughs brightly. 'It only just occurred to me I could go outside, actually.'

'I know what you mean. We eat together, go to sleep at the same time. It's really nice. But I forget I'm allowed to go buy a pack of gum outside of a group-haul shopping trip.' She pauses. Her hair is silvery in the dark. 'Is it okay if I come with you?'

Elen nods. She watches the sky as Lyn ducks back inside for a scarf and when Lyn reappears she smiles. They walk through the trees. Their conversation while walking occasionally lapses and then resumes without difficulty a few minutes later. After ten minutes they've reached the parkway, but it's quiet and moonlit and the grassy verges are walkable so they continue. The Rockies crawl alongside them; the sky above the Rockies seems to be drawn very thin. Cars are so infrequent that they can hear the river running somewhere below and to the side of the freeway, and Lyn moves closer every time they see highlights.

Elen knows where it's all from now: the blood overflowing in the sink, the surety with which she felt the truth of George's body in the stupid empty cupboard. These are the sister visions to ones she'd had years ago, of insects materialising on dirty dishes and of Robert, astral projected into the guesthouse, reaching out for her. They are symptoms of the falling apart that accompanies a certain kind of love, only now it's love in its first stages rather than its last.

But the agitation she's felt since dinner persists, even if she's pretty sure it's exclusively focused on the real stuff and not the ominous love-mad delusions. (The neon clothespins in their basket sparkle at her as another car passes.) If she's not worried about hallucinating blood and bodies, all that's left is the video of Luka's brother and the book of Luka's notes. Elen inhales and the breath is cold and sharp. If she stops worrying for a moment, she might be forced to admit that she's found it: the missing piece, the force driving Luka's commitment to the dream. And that it's not unsound. She's felt on the brink of something since she saw the video (the katana, the watermelon, the blood). Could it be called assurance into which she's teetering? Or called hope – confidence – conviction that she is with people who want what she wants. Elen thinks that hope might feel like this, like panic and calm and Lyn and the river. It might feel like this if Elen could accept that this life could be real, that it could last. Of course, something nags still. Lyn, drawing closer again, starts her next sentence a couple of times before she says it.

*

'This is nice,' she says eventually, looking straight ahead at the road. 'But I feel like maybe you wanted to be alone.' Lyn doesn't do rising intonations, but in case it wasn't clear that she'd asked a question, she follows up after ten seconds of silence. 'What's up with you?'

Elen frames a response in her head. There's only one thing now, chewing at the foundations of a prospective future in which she has new faith. The answer is clear and real, and pink and trashy. But in the face of this new faith, how can Elen go ahead and reveal herself suddenly to be the intruder? The guest gone bad, burrowing through their makeshift home after all their hospitality.

'I've been thinking about Luka.' When she speaks, it's slowly. 'I actually did a bit of Fourier reading.'

Lyn's reply is immediate. 'Ah, you've found it. His dirty pink secret.'

'The book?'

'The book.'

'I didn't mean to. I was looking for' (*Crampons*, her brain offered. What are crampons?) 'something else.'

'I'm sure he'd be genuinely pleased that you'd read it. All he wants is someone else to talk to about all of that. I read it a while ago and just couldn't make my way through it.' When Lyn talks about reading the book, she rolls up the sleeves of her sweater in a way that confirms that this is a sports girl. A British variant, but a soccer bitch nonetheless. But—

'But Lyn, did you see the notes in the margins?'

Lyn bursts out laughing. 'Oh, forgive him the notes, Elen.'

Elen's mind races ahead of her – could she laugh too, and in so doing, grab her hand? Could she seize the snowy red little hand? Red with the cold and almost violet in the evening. But it was bizarre that Lyn would pass over the notes.

They turn a corner of the parkway, and though they are still up on the grass they take it slowly. It's a sharp curve, almost hairpin, and a car coming round it wouldn't be visible until the very last minute. But on the other side only the moon bursts into view, suddenly, perfectly. Elen clicks her tongue, watches the moon bloom, works out how to phrase what she wants to say.

'I feel like you have him on a real pedestal. Those notes were so strange.'

(No, that wasn't how she wanted to say it.)

Lyn stills next to her. Here it comes, Elen thinks. Lyn is now the lone generator of that vague aura of insularity, exclusivity, which had once belonged to the teenagers, and she is still working overtime. But then she softens under the moon and yields.

'I think those notes are from at least a couple of years ago. Look, be honest with me. Are you worried about the sex stuff?'

Elen breaks. 'I am, you know. I am worried about the sex stuff. There was just so much sex stuff.'

They laugh together. 'Poor frustrated Luka. Be kind to him; it's just his way. He jacked off to a mountain, didn't you hear?'

'Oh, but there were other things.' Elen forces the laughter down. 'All the weird shit he'd underlined ... women and children. He's obsessed. And Fourier's obsessed! There are sketches of work uniforms, nursery furniture. The number of playwrights that he thinks Harmony would produce. The

Little Hordes of kids activated to do the phalanx's disgusting work. That's a quote, Lyn, "disgusting work." And Luka highlighted the part that said, "Judging modern women is like judging beavers in captivity."'

Lyn shrieks. It's unexpected and hilarious. 'The beaver thing, oh my god. I'd forgotten the beaver thing.' She grips Elen and they both are laughing, they both are nearly crying, the moon is large and close.

Elen muses. She still hasn't said what she wanted to. They are near where they keep the car parked, she realises. The route looks different at night-time. The mountain air is wide and clear, the view blurs under the moon. They stay, talking only a little bit, walking in circles; they pull each other out of the way of cars and every time they do they leave their hands on each other for longer. The two of them are there for a while and they are both there because they want to be.

Chapter 21

Elen stretches her sore legs past the corners of her child's bed. The warmth that had been there on the parkway yesterday is stuck to her still, like pollen. She draws the sensation up over her shoulders, over her head. Alone at 4 a.m. that morning, she had remembered again that liking someone meant feeling crazy, meant second guessing ... Coming loose at the edges in nights that were suddenly full of hours. Sometimes it meant seeing blood and hearing cupboards sing of the dead. And she doesn't mind. There's something between her and Lyn, lovely and unspoken. When – if – anything happens, they won't keep it from Luka. She's sure of that, but it doesn't trouble her. There are mountains to ski, there is unbelievable time. They will go to Turkey. For the first time, she believes without reserve that she will go to Turkey. What's Turkey? Sea and mosques and pottery, sunny domes, caves of ice. And mountains and snow for ever. Acid is just skiing in a tab!

+++

The quietest sound on the ground floor of Hanneke brings her down again.

Ever since seeing Clover's breast (like an egg) in George's mouth, Elen has been careful about doors. She knocks and she waits. So she does not accidentally walk in on Clover crying in the downstairs bathroom. In fact, when she hears the muffled, unmistakeable sighs, she turns the other way and does a lap of the house, knowing the whole time (on an osteal level) that the right thing, and the thing that she will do, is to check on her.

'Hey,' she says as she turns the doorknob. Clover looks up, wide eyed, surprised that the usual silence of her sobbing has failed her. Elen takes in the scene. It takes her a while to spot the surprise which ultimately reveals itself to be four pregnancy tests on the sink behind her. 'Oh, sweetie.' Elen reaches for her, strokes her hair. Clover stops crying and balls up some tissue in the hand that isn't pinching the top of her thigh.

Half a second later there's a knock at the door. They both start. One of the tests slides into the basin, like a joke. 'Can you give me a second?' Elen starts to say but the door's already opening. It's only Lyn, who slips in.

'What are you two doing? Oh fuck, fuck, fuck.' She apologises as soon as she's said it, as though actually the positive pregnancy tests could be construed as a good thing, a fun surprise, and she's put her sweary catastrophising spin on it too soon.

'I feel like a defective typewriter,' says Clover. Elen and Lyn look at each other, not understanding. 'Oh my god, of course you two don't know what I'm talking about. Where are all the fucking normal people?' She apologises then, and works herself up again, possibly this time just for snapping at them. They bow their heads over the *pisseux bâtons*. A bathroom is not a kitchen. The colluding done in a bathroom is rarely joyful.

'We're going to sort this,' says Elen, surprising herself. 'Whatever you want to do, we're going to sort this.'

'Please can we not tell Luka yet?'

Lyn winces. This one's a no-brainer for Elen but Lyn hears: secrets and lies. An almost marvellous thing: however increasingly human she seems, however affectionate she's become, that slight coolness never leaves her eyes. It's the colour of them.

'Right. But you've been skiing? You've been doing acid? You've been sliding down mountains? Is it even possible?'

'Please,' says Clover thickly. 'It's the size of a bean right now.' (Elen catches herself feeling grateful that Clover hadn't said a tonka bean, or whatever.) 'And I'm a great skier. And I didn't do acid.'

'Did you know then?' Lyn asks. 'Is that why you didn't take acid? Is that why George left?'

'I don't even know now,' says Clover quite ferociously. 'I'm going to take another test.'

'Do you have another test?'

'I'm going out to get one.' She stalks out the door. As Lyn and Elen file out behind her, Luka raises his head up solemnly from the sofa.

'Are you okay, Clover? Is there anything I can do?'

She looks afraid. 'Did you hear all that?'

He nods. 'Yes,' he says, gently. 'Of course I did.'

All at once, a peculiar tension drains out of Elen. Keeping secrets from Luka does feel terrible. More than that, having

Luka on side, with his energetic friendliness and upbeat efficiency, is in fact instantly reassuring. Especially given how bouncily solicitous he's being now, without deviating from the classic Luka way. 'Do you want a cigarette? Do you want a cup of tea? We'll sort this, Clove, I promise.' Elen's flooded by a rising respect for the boy. It's how she'd felt when they'd stopped at the vista on the acid day, and skied down from it together holding hands.

Until, of course, he breaks it. Just one rock through the window: 'I assume it's George's.' Said deliberately and without eye contact. The atmosphere falters and shifts from there. Clover goes and sits on the other sofa, lays her head back to look at the ceiling. Lyn slides imaginary dirt from out her fingernails.

Luka sets the cup of tea in front of Clover, who still won't look at him. He sits back down comfortably, ankle on knee, and says, 'Okay, okay, team. What are we going to do?'

'Do you want to let George know?' Lyn asks.

'We should. You know. If you want, I'll write the message and you can just press send.'

Clover nods, but this turns out to be ridiculous in practice. *'Hi George I'm pregnant. Not a joke.' 'Hi George, guess what? (emoji).'* It loosens Clover out in a way – not that she laughs, but her upset softens out into more of a gloom. What was it Luka had said after George had disappeared? 'This is when your dad goes to the shop for cigarettes and doesn't come back.' The house feels full of needles.

Elen trails over to the kitchen cupboards, takes a bottle out. They've been buying the brand they'd found the chalet stocked with. Rich kids. They're debating the merits of *Hi George I really need to talk to you about something urgent.* She doesn't need it like she often does, which is nice. But rolling the dark sediment over her tongue does make her feel better. Drinking doesn't have to be all or nothing, after all. She looks up and Luka is watching her.

'Good idea,' he says. 'Pour me one?' They've lived together for a month now. Elen has handed Luka things a hundred times – ski poles, cigarettes, coffee. But bringing the wine to him, red in its glass, feels loaded.

Once all of them are encamped on the couches, talk turns to the inevitable. When, and how, and would she have to go back to the UK to get an abortion?

'You'd be amazed at how many people have had them,' says Lyn. 'It's like one in three or something. I haven't.'

Clover looks sulky. She and Elen are the only ones who haven't said the word abortion yet, but the other two are now confidently tossing it back and forth. Every time Lyn says it, Elen thinks of Clover's face in the kitchen at midnight: wanting a baby, thinking it would be unethical to plan having one; scared of the end of snow. She tries not to look for any signs that maternal feeling has already manifested. It would be dumb to think that Clover once mentioning broody spells makes this situation any easier. She avoids the sight of Clover's hands and their proximity to her stomach. The dishes are undone. Elen notices that the feathery houseplant above the sink, which she'd assumed was fake, is starting to curl up. 'I haven't,' says Lyn again, 'But literally loads of people have.'

The message has been sent to George. It's obvious that they won't be skiing today so Luka sets another couple of bottles on the table where Clover's tea is going cold. He's back, the self-appointed king of libations, he's making sure each person has their drink with care. He even fills some glasses to make the choice more convenient for them. Lyn is talking at an uncharacteristic pace – about *Juno*, childcare, the abortions of her friends of friends. Clover checks her phone like a crazy person as the rest of them become more horizontal.

'No drink for you, girly?' Luka says to her. 'If you're going to get rid of it, a glass of wine really doesn't matter. It'll make you feel better,' he says, not kindly. Elen watches Clover's face translate her thoughts in slow motion.

'I'm really lucky to just view it as an extension of health-care ...' Lyn's clear voice surfacing as Clover looks into the glass. Can she see her own face in the dark? '... Obviously – like, naturally – some people think it's so deep, but that *is* such a burden. I feel very lucky, to be honest, for me the idea of an abortion is like taking insulin or getting a broken bone fixed.' Perhaps she means to cast aspersions on Americans, but it's Clover who bursts into thick tears.

Luka melts. He gathers her beautiful, beautiful hair in his plump hand as though she's throwing up rather than crying. 'Listen. Do you know why we're all feeling like this – sluggish and bad tempered? It's because we've not been skiing. I'm not even kidding. If exercise was a medicine, every doctor in the world would prescribe it.'

Clover laughs softly, leans her head in to his touch. 'Would it kill a foetus?'

He pets her. 'And that makes skiing a miracle pill – exercise plus immersion in the sublime.'

She sips at the wine, holding the glass in both hands like

a kid. Elen lets her head drop back into the sofa. Outside it's raining. Someone says they think that the Irish call it soft rain. Someone else, someone who hasn't stopped checking their phone, gets a news alert: there's been a flooding at River Lane.

'Where's River Lane?' asks Elen. 'Is that in Banff?'

'No,' says Clover, sheepish and teary. The Real Hippie is still set to receive news alerts for her little village in Kent. The wine's going to their heads; no one's eaten yet today. Hanneke is getting drizzled at the windows. The slopes will be icy tomorrow.

'You know,' Luka says, 'You could still do it. It's earlier than we planned but you could have a little phalanstery baby.' (Lyn laughs.) 'You're really special, Clove. Look how you look after all of us. You could raise him up, if you wanted to. And we'd help.'

Clover doesn't say anything.

'I reckon we need to go to Turkey. Bit more skiing until you're too big. And in Turkey, there's so much cross-country. It'll be totally safe, good for you. George will meet us there. He'll have to.'

She raises a glass to that. Elen closes her eyes to think about this. When she opens them, she sees the wine that she likes best is running low. She pours out the last of it while Luka describes how to ski pregnant in Turkey. ('Plus we need to go to Turkey soon. There's a seasonal imperative. It's like farming, ladies. It's like growing crops, and the crops are babies.') Clover isn't looking at him. During one of his deliberate, oratory pauses, Elen looks across at him and is shocked at how little his face matches his tone. For the first time since finding out, the comforting expression has slipped. It's back on by the next sentence, but that gap ...

There's something frightening about that kind of franticness on a face which at rest reminds Elen of no one so much as the stoner turtle from *Finding Nemo*. It had been the same unhidden panic that gunshots might elicit. It had been how he might have looked if he'd learned about George and Clover sleeping together before it was too late. Well, done right, the connection between a mother and child can be inalienable, Elen had heard. It's exclusive. He might never be able to reach Clover again. Perhaps Luka had been thinking that even if he looks past the obvious periods of pregnancy and post-partum and early child-rearing that would have her out of action, even if he thinks that he would actually still be able to bring her and her child back into to the fold, neither of them will ever truly be under his influence. Elen wonders who Luka thinks of when he thinks of children. Certainly not a nephew tucked into bed, shouting sleepily that he mustn't take his quail away. He's only a kid himself; maybe he's thinking of his own childhood, second fiddle to a younger brother who looked like him but was stronger and who hit people across the head with charisma. She swallowed the wine. This was harsh. There were other lights in which Luka would consider children. From a Fourierian perspective, it would not be bad for the phalanx; it's a big milestone for a cult, getting the kids in. And children are connected to a mysterious world, a sublime world, which after all was a part of what Luka was chasing: a world of imagination. They were to be envied and encouraged – we are closest to angels when we are born, and then we grow older. For all Elen knew he might have wanted

Clover's baby to serve as one of the little medieval hermit kids kept at courts by libertine kings to pray for them.

'The thing is, we actually do need to go to Turkey soon. The season's basically over. The window's perfect – all the tourists are gone, for sure, but there's still snow on the ground. But not for long.' He makes eye contact with each of them, one after the other, as he delivers this, and his expression is immaculate.

'Luka's actually so right.' Lyn is fully horizontal now, pointing her toes towards her and her heels away. Elen can feel the stretch in her own feet. They haven't looked at each other much today, what with all the drama. She remembers last night's closeness. It's like something that happened two months ago. 'I worked it out a while ago; the window is closing. Even at altitude, the snow will be gone before the end of May. If we leave tomorrow we can get maybe two weeks.'

'I didn't realise we'd been here so long,' Clover says. She's tired. She turns the phone off and on again absently, pours herself another glass of wine. She's not drunk, but the others are approaching it. Elen's approaching it. She looks at Lyn bending her feet forward and backward. She thinks about having woken up in the same room as her in Bend every day for weeks; seeing her fresh faced and pressing the small, wing-shaped *gua sha* stone into the arches of her white feet. So that she might lay them better upon the mountain. Lyn is pretending to be oblivious to her now. Leaping on the idiot bandwagon of Let's get out of here, Let's go to Turkey. Elen's seen the crazy, genius precision of those maps; there's no way Luka has let the window close. He wants to requisition

Clover, requisition her baby for the Little Hordes. Elen feels that her bones are soft and blurry inside their limbs.

Brave of Luka to resurrect his vision even as he sees his clan crumbling before his eyes. Perhaps he does believe George will come charging back to Turkey to be a part of their mountainside Camelot. Sea and mosques and pottery. Fairy-tale stuff.

Chapter 22

Elen isn't sure if they sent her out to get more drinks or if she at some point volunteered to go, but she's got Clover's jacket on and is crossing the ring of fir trees that surround the house. The soft rain has petered out into a mistiness. The air is bracing, sort of sobering. She imagines that she is hiking uphill, against the wind and into the snow, though she's just following the footpath that leads into Banff.

Every building in Banff is built like a chalet, low and some-how ye-olde. Even the bank has a timber exterior wall. It's further than she'd thought, though she doesn't have to go into the town proper. She's only ever been through in the car; they have a Starbucks there, and a Tim Hortons, a Museum of the Canadian Rockies and a store just for 'Mountain Chocolates'. But there's a lone convenience store further out towards the Airbnb. When she steps inside, she can hear all the fridges buzzing.

The cashier is bald and tall. Extremely so. As though in both aspects he's one degree away from some condition, alopecia or gigantism. Or she is drunk. Or this is simply the effect of seeing a person who wasn't one of the teenagers;

small differences being heightened cartoonishly. Elen realises that she's been staring. The cashier wasn't frightening, but it was frightening how much seeing a new person felt like coming up for air.

She wanders through the breadsticks, biscuits, the cartoon mascots of the cereal aisle. The endcap is full of green floats. When she looks closer she sees that they are packs of diapers. Babies at various ages sleep, crawl and walk on the boxes. Elen is examining the rubric seriously – promised level of dryness, baby age, appropriate grip around said baby's sides – before she remembers that she hasn't actually been sent to get diapers. The cashier is staring at her. No, no one's staring at her. The last time she was sent out to get diapers it was for Lee.

That had been a wonderful time, actually, welcoming a baby that wasn't hers into the family. Banding around Susannah, running errands and talking seriously about temperatures, then going home before the sleepless, screaming nights were in full swing. Elen had made a casserole for the first time in her life. 'You were born to be an aunt,' Robert had told her. It had been a compliment.

Lee is growing into a good kid, or had been when Elen left Bend. Being kind to animals was one of those things you were supposed to look for in children, wasn't it? One of those things that proved that they wouldn't grow up into a serial killer or melon-slasher. And Lee more or less saved quails from the slaughter. He's a good kid. He's being brought up around mountains. He didn't speak French or know about Greek myths and Fourier like the little cult-raised child of Clover's old dreams, but they had a positive effect, the mountains. He made his own cross-country skis from a kit when he was five and sometimes she would catch him cloud-watching of his own accord. Elen takes four bottles of wine, one of gin, and one of tonic to the till and pays with Luka's card. She wonders vaguely how much is left in her emergency account.

'Thank you,' she says to the cashier, trying to put the full weight of what she means into the words.

'No problem,' he smiles. 'Have a lovely day.'

When she gets back to the Airbnb, she finds that the couch-drinking has devolved, or been elevated. Clover is tipsy rather than weepy. Luka is standing on the sofa and inhaling the last drops of wine from the old bottle, like a Russian who has happily escaped the revolution. His head is very close to the ceiling. Lyn helps Elen unload the bottles, and puts the back of her hand on Elen's cheek.

'What was that for?' says Elen, surprised. She hadn't noticed the rain on the way back until Lyn points out the thin layer of wet on her skin.

'Aha! Elen! Look!' Luka points at his wrist where he is not wearing a watch. 'It's 4 p.m. Do you know what that means? It's après time.' Elen looks to Lyn so that they can exchange 'this doesn't bode well' faces, but Lyn is looking up at Luka like a devotee and he continues as if he's reciting the beatitudes. 'Let's put on après music. Clover, go!' It seems that Clover knows what this means. She refreshes her messages one last time, blinks heavily, and then puts her phone into an empty glass. The song that starts playing resounds spookily through the castellations. It sounds like an electronic remix of German yodelling. 'And now shots. Shots. Jägerbombs. Beers.'

'I have gin and tonic,' says Elen, holding up the bottles.

'That will do!'

The German yodelling, she finds, is surprisingly easy listening if you're drunk. At some point in the next hour, a curious sensation knocks her. It feels like a wave has passed through her body. It's the smell of indoor cigarette smoking, she realises, which has conjured the presence of George so strongly that he might as well have walked through the door. They're smoking inside. This is bad news in a borrowed house. The smoke will attack the fabrics. Luka's never let them smoke inside before. He thinks like a landlord: no spills, no shed hair, no smoking inside, nothing that could lower the resale value or give away that they were ever there. But now he's leading the charge, swaying on the sofa with a full wine glass. Elen notices things like a landlord too when she's looking for evidence of a family once having lived here: grout in the tiling, glitter in the cracks in the furniture. A handprint left in cheap foundation, barely noticeable, on the white paint underneath the banister. Even now, it's her watching the smoke curl into the walls and thinking – we'll be found out. Luka's just still doing his impression of a teenage girl at après. 'Oh my god. Like. Let's. Get. Some. Poutine.'

It feels like an après. She remembers the party in the haunted resort – not a party, a 'beers'. Swinging coloured lights, back when swinging coloured lights were enough to turn the teenagers' faces into something weird and unfamiliar to Elen. Now she'd recognise them in the dark. It had been a great night. They'd been celebrating Elen deciding to stay. *Toad-Hall-Whistler,* George had said, and then there'd been an orgiastic gleam. But now she mainly remembers George rolling Clover a cigarette, Clover with her arms around him, cheek to cheek, everyone happy. Love, skin soft. Its own guest. She turns around on the spot, thinking maybe Lyn will roll her a cigarette. But Lyn is drunk like Elen's never seen her: youngly drunk. Clover and Luka are huddled on the sofa and Lyn is dancing in the middle of the room. 'You can call her Hanneke,' Luka is saying, pissed. 'We had a good time here, didn't we? We have a good time.'

And now the front door is open and Lyn and Clover are sitting in the doorway. Lyn has her arm around Clover. The night presses in at them. Wasn't it 4 p.m. a minute ago? Only the very first trees are illuminated by the light from inside the house. Everything else is black. Elen's been sweating but the rush of cold air is too cold. She wants to wash her hands. Lyn and Clover are talking excitedly at each other, loud and drunk. There is no way or reason to join them. Elen goes to find Luka who will get everyone on their feet, get the night started again.

She runs into him on the landing, coming out of the upstairs bathroom.

'How goes it?' He's smashed. She presents the wine bottle she's holding, meaning Let's Keep Going. 'Oh, Elen,' he says, smiling, taking it. 'Never before have I ever met someone who just so totally gets it.'

'Thank you.'

He slides to the floor of the landing and she joins him, legs straight out in front of her. It's weird to look at him with her new knowledge. She and Luka are not alike, but they've both seen the contract of family flouted. They take turns sipping the wine, Luka talking about what a gift it was to find her, how much everyone adores her, how much better she fills out their little group than George ever did.

It's curious, this thing he does. This weird sweet-talk, which is objectively ingratiating ('You're a gorgeous girlie, you're the best, I hope you're coming to Turkey because I'd follow you to the end of the earth'), but which hits a spot, because of his earnest boyishness or because you're feeling low. It works for Clover – she leans in to the hand in the pony-tail, still blushes when he calls her 'a beautiful real-life flower child.' He didn't used to turn it on George too much, but it was just Luka and the women now. Elen nodding and rolling the wine in her mouth and thinking about those who were most vulnerable to terrorist recruitment or visions of utopia. How is it that Lyn stands it, is entertained by it?

She's still thinking about Lyn when they kiss. When the Lyn thoughts make way for the realisation that they're kissing, it feels like she's come to. They've changed positions, which is to say that Luka is now in front of her where before he was to her left but also that they're no longer in the hallway. It takes Elen a second to place herself. The moisturisers give it away; she's surrounded by them – they seem to have multiplied. Some stand empty, some roll on their side as if wounded. She moves apart from him only after a new intrusion by his tongue.

'Are you good?' he asks her, letting her pull away but not reply. 'Yeah, you're good, you're good.'

'How long have we been ...' she gestures to the space between them.

'Like ten minutes. You're a good kisser,' he says, in the

same way that he says, 'Clover, you're looking beautiful today.' Flippant, void of significance, almost comforting. Elen lets him move his mouth back over hers, not thinking much. She slides a hand under his shirt.

Everyone gets with everyone during periods of intense transition. Sometimes drunkenness is its own period of transition. Could that be true? Kissing Luka is kind of like acid in that it's constant short-term memory loss – a loop of forgetting what she's doing and realising and shocking and then rationalising it to herself. The dream-state blur effect (that time-lapse montage of mouth-mouth, mouth-neck, hand-shoulder, hand-breast, hand-stomach) is a long-forgotten thing. It had been during that period of missing Liberty, back in Michigan and just out of school, when Elen had been less adjusted to drinking, which was not to say drinking less. She would regularly end the night in a surprising bed, confused as to how she got there, moving in ways that were more energetic than usual. When something like that happens you put the clues together. You remember saying yes but not why. You remember seeing the leather jacket across the bar five hours ago, but not where the boxes of takeout had come from. The willingness to continue is indistinguishable from the unwillingness to fuss, and the faint embarrassing memory, real or imagined, of at one point being very enthusiastic all means deciding that you can't stop a train which you know, in your bones, even if you don't remember, you had so dementedly set in motion. These had all been familiar rituals to Elen, only a couple of years before she'd married Robert.

Now, as then, the alcohol has her loose and sexual. She's still thinking of Lyn. Glimpses of a naked back and shoulders in the morning. Lying next to her in the resort, with Clover on the other side of the room. Not daring to open her eyes while she could hear Lyn undressing and getting into bed. Not daring to open her eyes but knowing that their bodies were laid out side by side – not opening her eyes, but envisioning that soft-focus bird's-eye view where it would appear that they were sharing a bed, or grave. Not opening her eyes, but moving into the kiss … and then, suddenly, Elen finds that she couldn't open her eyes even if she wanted to.

'Are we downstairs?' she asks. She has an awful feeling that the two of them are kissing downstairs, among the afghans, that Clover and Lyn are with them, drunk, looming over them, laughing, watching. The electro-yodelling has stopped. If Clover and Lyn are in the room they are very quiet. Everything is very quiet: mountain quiet. She can hear Luka's breathing, and her own.

'Still no,' Luka says. 'Still upstairs.'

She opens her eyes. The moonlight in the girls' room hides nothing, only softens. Luka is over her. His skin is so smooth. Tan, and hairless, like a boy's. His nipples are oddly high on his chest. There's a leap, she realises; a big stretch of missing time between everyone drinking downstairs and then Elen's trip upstairs to find him. She is an empty house. He moves easily inside her. She tries to recall.

'*You can call her Hanneke,*' Luka was saying, and Lyn was tapping Elen on the back of her wrist.

'Are you okay?' Elen said.

'You're nice,' said Lyn happily.

Nice was a word much disassociated from cold-column

Lyn, with all her rejection of the comfortable in favour of the sublime. But Elen wasn't going to think too hard about it.

'Thank you,' she said. She was nice. They were dancing.

She kept drinking. She remembered whatever Lyn had said when they were sharing the Bombardino. She was a heavyweight, a heavyweight champ. She remembered when Lyn had said that she'd started feeling numb after university, anaesthetised. Whatever Lyn was running away from it was working. Her hair floated out from her neck in time with the music, like static in slow motion. But Elen couldn't think about Lyn's cool neck without thinking of where in the room Luka and Clover were and then she spotted Clover and thought about the meaninglessness of this all having happened right now. There was no use trying to get inside Clover's head. Clover had something growing inside her, doubling and doubling; surely she'd be thinking about that? But she was on the couch, eyes closed, snapping her fingers just off beat. And Lyn danced and Elen drank and Elen remembered something that George had said. She'd been talking about getting fucked up and he'd been talking about Greek tragedies. Oh, he should have saved it for their Tudor princeling, their little ski prodigy in his woollen doublet! Tragedy, George had said, never happened when you were fucked up, but always when you were sober. They would get totally inebriated, the Ancient Greeks, and they would do terrible things: steal livestock, kill their parents, tear the heads and limbs off their kids. But these were only formally tragedies at the point of anagnorisis, George had said, and Elen had asked him what that meant, because that was her part to play. 'It becomes a tragedy when the mother asks whose bloody head she's holding and they tell her it's her son's. The sobering up is the tragedy.' Elen had nodded, like, yeah.

She wouldn't shift Clover, whose eyes were now open but unfocused. She was nice. In a moment, Lyn would pull Clover to sit in the open doorway so that they could talk a while, and Elen would take that as her cue. But for now Lyn was just dancing. The oven hood light was on, a couple of candles were lit. Lyn was spinning, turning her arms, warm, happy.

Chapter 23

Elen used to wonder if she might have sensed it, Robert's vanishing in the night. Some part of her had registered the moment, she suspected. The ragged kind of sleep that's brought on by drinking, plus the thin walls and close quarters of her old house: would she not have heard something? Would she not even have rolled over at the door closing, thinking she'd dreamed it?

Asleep now in Canada, in the upstairs room of a stolen house, it's that same thin sleep, pierced every time the moon comes out from behind a cloud or the body beside her shifts in the bed. Vanishing in the night from Hanneke would be hard to obscure. When George had managed it they'd all been curled up in the front room, shattered from visions. The bed creaks. Elen's sleep draws thinner: it endures, but her eyes are moving quick behind their lids. Movement in the room corresponds to sleep spindles, peaks and troughs of sudden thought, ideas reshaping and consolidating in the pitching dreamy gauze.

She is seeing something in the palpebral tissue. When Robert had vanished the possibilities were various, exploded. The images of him changed country and outfit with every involuntary flutter of her eyelids. The image that now arrives is just one. It's inevitable; she realises it as she dreams it. Whatever minorly differentiated ways there might have been for him to get there, this is where he is. George, the lost member of the lunatic tertulia.

Here, moonlight washes vaguely over a corner of Elen's face but There it's light and early, not quite daybreak. Steam comes off the water of a blue rectangle and disappears in the cold. To the side of the swimming pool there's a bench – no, she thinks; there's a small, bridal-looking gazebo, she's certain, and it's empty. Both pool and hut are encompassed by a thin brambly hedge, beyond which the rest of the grounds stretch for acres. And there he is: George, swimming long quiet lengths in his parents' pool.

He comes up for air at the end of each length. The rest of the time, he doesn't break the water. The pale body popples, broad and freckled, rolling underneath the misty surface like some kind of creature. His phone has been off since he got back; it's somewhere at the bottom of his suitcase, somewhere in the corner of his bedroom. The creature has not received any of his friends' texts.

Some brave greenery makes its way out from between two paving stones; thistles, something that might be called lamb's lettuce. They are flooded without thought when George pulls himself out of the water. Maybe he shakes his head like a dog, maybe he grabs a towel; whichever it is, everything's cool, careless. Elen's muscles twitch in concert with him, one hypnic jerk. It looks like she's practising jumps in her sleep.

It's early. It's cold. The silence is total but for his flat wet feet and the lapping pool. No birds. Thick white cloud cover.

He doesn't put dry clothes on to sit in the gazebo, just keeps the towel round his rosy, freckled shoulders, and his nipples pucker, his chest goes ruddy. He takes the lid off a Thermos, puts his mouth against the metal mouth and inhales the steam. Too hot to drink. Staring into space, he flubs his lips against the rim like a baby. That's allowed, surely, still in the grip of jet lag. Thinking about the airport, the rushed tedium of the flights, his dad's voice methodical on the phone is like thinking about a break-up, crystal girl, the memories form a kind of traumatic supercut. But Elen knows that he can remember the last day with his friends perfectly – frame by frame. He's thinking something about *all the bloody Greek letters on the trees* and then Luka's voice, his best friend's voice, will have done its old magic trick, drawing pictures.

(The understanding of what's happened is singular, undeniable. Elen can't hear either's voice. Her unconscious cogitation stays soundless except for the wet feet, the pool. She can see Luka's voice instead – he's unfurling his vision, as per, giving it some air: a utopia with spires better than Oxford's and a covered courtyard like at school. George has laughed. She can't hear this either: she can see George, live from the gazebo, remembering the laugh and simultaneously she can see all her own memories of his laughing overlapping, twenty red brays. Whatever the various permutations are of the conversation, this is what it looks like: Luka earnest, George thoughtless, blithe, calling Fourier 'Marie or whatever', and Luka's dawning realisation that the future doesn't look like spires and courtyards to George.

He's always been the odd one out. He's never truly deviated from expecting a normal life, a life in what Luka calls civilisation. He's never felt the draw that Luka, Lyn, Clover have, that Elen has; he's just a boy who loves his friends. Elen's understanding all this in her sleep so when she unlocks George's disappearance there's no shock or dread, no sudden scary movie comprehension, just the sliding into place of things that are obviously, patently true.

The tragedy of George's disappearance is not, as waking-Elen had thought, that he'd run out on Clover in the spur of the moment, that he'd vanished in the night, that he hadn't felt beholden to the girl who loved him; nor is it the tragedy of road accidents or Dyatlov Passes. It's the tragedy of prac-ticality. The disparity, in practice, of visions and friendships: the incompatibility, in practice, of utopia and humans. Or: Luka, yearning vs. George, content.)

In the gazebo George is wondering how Luka has ration-alised away his disappearance. He knows him so well! He contemplates the potential lies with genuine curiosity. Elen dreams that his fingers are itching for the rolling papers. His guesses will be rational: that his mother had called with a sickness or maybe the old Irish goodbye or maybe something horrible: a car crash, an avalanche. These are more unlikely but something in him relishes the irony of the second image – his ski-suited body crushed under heaps of fallen snow. Elen is sure, as the sleeping are always sure. An avalanche's only right, he's thinking, working up some line like *Belief in the natural world as an antidote to modernity must end in symbolic failure. Death at the hands of natural disaster.* Ah, but he was only in it for his pals. She knows the cadence of his talk so well. Asleep, she sees the young voice like an old friend. He amuses himself looking at antique facts from every angle and offers up the ones of which he's proudest under the cover of quip. *It was the Greeks who'd invented ostracism as a way of neutralising threats to the state*, he'll be thinking now. *Any citizen could be expelled from Athens for ten years after the votes had been counted. No charge was needed, and no defence could be mounted.* Asleep, the shape of these facts come to Elen because she knows what he knows.

He's never been that interested in what's ahead. He likes the cities that have been and gone and are buried. The only thing he'd been running from was having nothing to run from, and now that's over he'll be fine doing nothing again, living with his parents, observing small shifts in circumstance with faint surprise – variations in girlfriends and then later in addresses or occupations, but minor variations each time. Nothing so out of left field as this again; he'd ticked it off the list. Arrested development is a kind of ghosthood. Elen feels this in her sleeping muscles, another hypnic twitch as someone passes in or out of the room in which she sleeps. Living the same life – there's a stagnancy of the air, a stasis of the blood. Those same eternal circuits, whether of home-pool-gazebo in England or home-guesthouse-brewery in Oregon, the tracks a ghost makes in a haunted house. The picture of George is so clear to her now. Gravely, he tilts the Thermos to his mouth, hi-res in her eyelids' black backs. He'll sit there for ever, thinking about the Greeks and modernity and friendship and Athenian debate in his parents' pool house, with the flat fields behind him and the sky white.

Chapter 24

Here catches up with There until it's early, not quite day-break. The sun must just be beginning to come up over the mountains. Some small light is just now reaching the house. There are different daybreaks, technically. Civic daybreak, nautical daybreak, astronomical daybreak or something like that. The sort of thing Lyn would know about, Elen thinks, even as she comes to in Luka's sweater. Without getting out of the bed or even raising herself up, she wriggles it off herself. Bare breasted in the cold bed she closes her eyes again.

The light used to come like this into her house in Bend. She and Robert would be woken up by it. They would wake up together. On the weekend, in the old days, he would go and make the coffee and then come back to bed. She'd loved the feeling of his warmth returning to the bed and the two separate warmths of their coffee cups waiting on the painted side table. She would burrow under the covers. They were pink with a ribbon seam that Elen remembers being able to pull all the way out of the fabric. A design flaw. She would give him head until he was just about to finish and then she would get out from under the covers and drink the coffee he'd made her and laugh at his frustration. And then she would relent. On the weekend, in the old days, they would *do* things: walk to Mirror Pond in the fall, have his brother's family round for lunch. One morning he brought her up a French stick cut into ten rounds with every kind of spread – peanut butter, chocolate spread, cream cheese, honey – and he wasn't hurt when she refused to make crumbs in the bed. They ate it downstairs, and there were crumbs everywhere anyway; he licked three off her cheek, and then they got clean together in their little shower that sputtered. Had that been one morning or every morning?

She tries to stay thinking about it – the memory of light which had shone through her old house is a balm to the rising hangover brought on by the beginnings of light in this one. But whatever had woken her up is still in the room. The fact of being in a home that's not her own, and the fact of another person making sounds by her head: both loom at the edge of Elen's consciousness like something shadowy in the fronds. She had seen a carp once in Mirror Pond that was almost vertical. Face up, behind the frog-bit, tail pointing down to the pond bottom. The fish never came to the surface, just floated in the dark dirt suspension, watching all the creatures in the light above. The gaping toothless hole in the middle of it seemed like a prehistoric threat, especially in contrast to the cutesy clapboard houses across the water, but Robert had pointed and said something about the redundancy of Susannah's Fish Passage Panel and Elen had laughed and loved him. She pushes now against the looming and the old house's remembered light washes over her and the warm light from an earlier time pushes through.

*

The lakes in Michigan were full of light. With her legs dangled in the water it seemed that clear light was rippling underneath and above them. They'd visited sometime during the first year of dating. It had felt like a honeymoon. She didn't know them well – she didn't know anywhere well, she'd spent twenty-one years only really moving between her hometown and Lansing, but Robert showed them off to her like a riviera.

Elen had wanted him so badly at first. They say that men fall in love quicker, and they say that women always make the first move without anyone knowing, simply by gesturing with their eyes across a room. But Elen had never seen either of these borne out. Men love second and longer, she found. She had waited for his call. She had shocked herself thinking of him so much. During that first year of dating in Michigan she'd even volunteered it to her mother – that she was in love – and her mother hadn't said much, unused to confidences, but she was pleased. She'd had an inkling of Elen's previous inclinations. The hangover takes hold of her temples – looms, watches – but she is thinking about being married three years into the new millennium and it was spring then and nothing loomed at all.

The hard, joyful year in Michigan of saving; the idea of moving to Oregon to join his brother, who she'd met just before the wedding when he'd been young and almost handsome. When they finally moved to Bend, into the house that they would live in for fifteen years, Elen and Robert did everything together. They even cooked together before his circuits of Work then Home then Sleep became more deeply grooved. Neither were good cooks, and they were regularly disappointed that what they'd thrown together in a pan hadn't been made more delicious by their shared joy at the throwing. The disappointment was eased by drink, by kisses, by the taste of skin and hair.

Oh, this point on the river: the last point before you can't look back. The treeline closes in on itself around the vanishing strait. Just before the view diminishes into nothing, it comes into focus. Imminent disappearance makes every reed sing, outlines every wavelet in indelible silver. A perspective illusion: the wing colours of distant birds are suddenly vivid. She'd met Robert at a club.

If she were awake, Elen would want this reminiscence to underline how totally ordinary Robert is, despite his hold over her. Why are paunchiness and baldness always signifiers for normal? When they met, Robert was totally normal, with short hair, and a flat, un-muscled stomach. He was dancing badly, he got her name wrong first time. But all this she glossed over – it had been loud in there. She'd been entranced. The dissolution of her relationship with Liberty, plus three months of jadedly sleeping around, meant that Elen was youthfully, philosophically sure that it was better to be the one who loved more. Robert believed in God, which tickled her. She isn't sure if he does still. She hopes he does. Deeply asleep, she hopes he does.

He'd slept with her so carefully that night after the club. It had basically been his first time. At least, it had been the first time he was allowed to finish inside. Elen kept that thought close to her for some years, imagining it gave her some power. Robert had always leapt from clearly having no power over her to having all of it, and then back. He could pick her up and put her on his shoulders. Their power over each other ebbed and flowed: they were ecstatically close and then completely detached. In the end he'd tipped the scales completely. Or freed her. He vanished – so she gets a vanishing; he took her youth, she'll crawl back into it. He prevented her from finding another woman to love ... Ah, there's no use thinking figuratively. There's no code.

The initial coursing feelings of love for Robert back in Michigan had also signalled the first time that Elen had cared about her hair, which was unbeautiful and short. Part of being gay was feeling that she didn't have to care. Loving a boy was easier in some ways and confusing in others. Once they'd moved to Bend she realised that she didn't care about her hair again. She didn't envy the teenagers, not even Clover for her beautiful hair: they all still cared. Lyn had the beginning of that unbotheredness but still checked for her own reflection in car windows. (Inside the car, behind the dark windows – someone, looming, watching.) Love had freed her from caring. Robert's love had freed her. Yes, the ordinariness leaked in for them both – he stopped cooking with her, she stopped wearing lipstick. But neither minded. She licked his armpit when he hadn't showered in days and didn't miss the cologne from the courtship era. There was a strip of skin that ran from below the armpit hair to where his dorsal muscle rippled into softness which she thought spectacular. She knew it as perfectly as she knew how he would respond to any given joke on any given day; she was as surprised by it as she was surprised by the way he handled things that went missing, a calm that was staggering after fifteen years together. The marriage paradox: you know someone down to their bones and not at all. Still they would be tangled up on the brown leatherette sofa and he would deliver a line of the song that she'd been thinking of a minute before. And she would lay her feet in his lap. A song could last between them for a month, spoken line by line.

She can see the brown leatherette sofa now. As though he were sitting on it. They'd had sex all over that house once, years ago. She'd brushed his teeth, he'd painted her nails, they'd fed each other, done press-ups on each other's backs. Elen can see the house now, spangled with their old motions. She moves through it, room by room: the kitchen window which looks onto the guesthouse and then the mountain; back into the house; the little bathroom where he held her hair back; the staircase here, the curtains there; the painting she found in a skip and him putting her on his shoulders to hang it. The old hiding spaces for bottles rattle at the fringes of her vision too. She moves through the rooms like a ghost. Robert is sitting on the sofa, or somebody else is. In a flicker of light through a bottle on the table she appears to them. *Disseisor.* Dispossessor.

Time blurs as Elen looms through the house. It accretes like an icefield. It coalesces around the curtains, paintings, bottles. The house is light, defined by the darkness which is not-house outside of it. A cube of light, with a stem of light for the chimney. The light is all of those irised gobbets that make up a marriage: mornings (pink), afternoons (blue), evenings (yellow), nights (cool), time together, time apart, meals, weekdays, weekends. They'd lived in Bend for more than fifteen years. Before the guesthouse conversion, before the drinking, he had loved her nose so much he'd put his mouth around the tip and sucked it like a nursing baby and then been surprised at the snot landing on his tongue. She knew she was not beautiful and he made her forget. 'What do you do?' 'I was a wife.' Before that even, she was in love.

+++

This is the part Elen used to dread, the sobering up. It's the sobering up that's the tragedy. The things you grieve for that aren't death, all at once. But whatever had woken her up is coming closer and closer. So she opens one eye and, fearing Luka, is relieved to see Clover. Clover's busy; she's cleaning up, collecting loose socks and bottle tops from under the bed. She's doing a good job; the room looks bare.

It's still not daybreak. Elen doesn't think she's ever seen Clover at this time before. Clover's a good sleeper usually, sweet like a child (with a silk eye-mask and Italian drying cream at the whorls of her nose). She looks fresh, even now. Elen dreads the sobering up more than the blackout but Clover makes a ritual of the morning after that rivals the bacchanal itself. One must, she seems to say. In soft, fresh clothes, and sore in the mouth from gnashing, one must pad gently down to set things right. Stock the dishwasher, make tea. Little gestures of absolution. Empty the ashtrays. Slay the Nemean lion. Bottles in the bin, blood in the sink.

Elen thinks perhaps Clover will look at her with sympathy, but Clover looks at her with an expression she's never seen before.

'I want to go to the hospital,' she tells Elen. 'Will you come with me?'

'Yes, of course. We'll all come with you.'

'They've gone,' says Clover.

No.

'They've left the house in a tip.'

'They wouldn't go without saying goodbye.' Elen is shocked at the voice that comes out of her own mouth. The sound of it is from some disaster movie. Even when Robert left she had never said aloud something so trite, something so obviously untrue.

'They left five minutes ago.'

For a long moment it seems that that's all that the new, steely Clover will say. But certain graces are impossible to unlearn. 'Do you want a cup of tea or something?'

'No.' Elen realises that she's naked under the bedclothes. 'Oh. Maybe some paracetamol.'

She's not a ghost any more or, at least, she's returned from the dead. The theatrical comeback in broad day! Her body is real and it's her own and so, once more, her actions have consequences. The consequences this morning are a hammering nausea and a second heartbeat in her head; paracetamol would actually be very welcome. Plus it's easier for Clover to talk with her back turned, rummaging through her Kaffe-Fassett-by-Coach washbag, letting Elen change.

'He booked the flight last night,' she says, 'Drunk. And said they had to take it. Or they'd be over-budget, basically. I think he said that it would throw off the totally balanced phalanstery economy but I might have imagined that one. He said his piece. That he'd catch the last of the Turkey snow and then come back for me. He was very clear on that.'

'Friendship's important to him.'

'I don't want to see him ever again.' Clover turns around. 'I only have ibuprofen.'

'And Lyn too.'

'Of course. She didn't say anything to me. Oh.' Her beautiful hair is scooped up like a wife's. 'They said they knew you'd help me get to the hospital. That they weren't leaving me alone, they were leaving me in good hands. That you are – good hands.'

Elen knows that she will. The trip has come to an end: there's always a sobering up. She doesn't think about Lyn but reaches stiffly up and holds Clover in an awkward hug for a while. For a long time, Elen had thought that she could do without people; that she didn't mind being alone, that she liked it even. She's no longer convinced that's true.

'Give me a minute and I'll drive you to the nearest hospital,' she says.

'They're taking the car,' replies Clover, in the same neutral tone.

Elen's good hands are shaking. Maybe it's the hangover. 'I'll be back. Give me twenty minutes.'

The air outside Hanneke is cool and clean from all the rain yesterday. It feels green against her face. The ring of fir trees seems suddenly as wide as a forest, or a country, but she is moving through them very fast – they left five minutes ago! – and she is thinking of her car, the car she'd left in Bend. Rusting, iced over, filled with her stuff, left behind. Items in its trunk appear to her. A pair of boots. A blue cushion: the only soft furnishing she'd saved from home, taken with the intention of having at least one thing she liked at her parents' house with her. Full of rage she starts running.

The route is the same one she walked with Lyn two days before. Elen's going at a speed that would have killed her in Bend but now the freeway is disappearing with ease underneath her new ski muscles. This will have been how George went, she thinks; these kids love to leave. She thinks all the crazy things you do think when you're running hard. She thinks about being sick, she thinks about stopping, about whatever she once knew of anaerobic respiration. Still, her speed doesn't let up. Elen's faster than she's been in years; she's been rewilded like Robert and the kids. But she won't live like them, like ghosts, beholden to nothing. Arrested development is a kind of ghosthood; at the same time, moving constantly is like not moving at all, and she's done both, sleeping in a child's trundle bed, hanging with kids as old as she'd been on her wedding day. The travelling utopia is only another kind of ghosthood, those undead who must roam the earth. Never settling is only a stasis-in-motion.

The thing in Elen that was still and dead for so long and then unsettled and made alive and set in constant motion had come to a rest in the bed with her that night. She runs hard down the road now and knows that she can be still again, as long as that thing's beating. What had woken up in her legs opens its eyes, restores itself to her body fully.

+++

The snow is melting when Elen starts the walk back towards Hanneke.

She'd only caught up with them because Luka had stopped

to admire the view. Poor Luka, foiled by his love for a good vista. There'd been a silence, cut with the river flowing somewhere under the freeway and the sound of her breathing returning to normal, and the air had been soft, as though wet. They'd all stopped in the middle of the road, all faced each other, standing at the sharp turn that she'd reached once before with Lyn; the hairpin, the farewell bend, where the moon had bloomed suddenly into view like a car coming round the corner.

Lyn had asked her to leave with them and she'd said no; Luka had asked her why she'd come, and she'd told them: only to witness their going. Only to disallow their vanishing in the night. They made a good couple. Elen only clocked it then, seeing them for the last time, side by side against a sweep of blue water which is even now flowing into the Vermilion Lakes. A stage magician and his assistant. They had done her a favour – thrilled her, shown her magic. You don't follow a magician home.

Luka's shadow had disappeared round the hairpin bend without pause. Lyn had stopped, turned around right where the road vanished into verge.

Perhaps she's still standing there. Some people can make a whole city out of the last point before you can't look back. But Elen keeps walking, through the melting snow.

Acknowledgements

Thank you to Amy Baxter, a wonderful friend, committed literary activist, and perfect editor. Thanks also to my agent, Matthew Marland, who encouraged me back when I was still working on a very ambitious campus novel.

More thanks are due to Nicky Allt, for giving me my first paid job in the world of literature, to Caroline Lamotte Pinheiro Lima for making me feel so at home in São Paulo, where I finished my final redraft, and to the London Writers Awards for their support. In particular, Lit Fiction B, who engaged with this book when it was still a short story – Tommy Rowlands, Sukh Brar, Cecile Pin, Shereen Akhtar, and Victoria Cano, thank you!

Finally, thank you to Caitlin Allt and Liza Hartley, for their constant love and inspiration; to Ben (Nohr), without whom my writing year would have been far less happy; to Indy, the first person I let read this, for her unvarying (and loving) honesty.

And to Dad again, for being a home I never doubted.

Bringing a book from manuscript to what you are reading is a team effort.

Dialogue Books would like to thank everyone who helped to publish *Winter Animals* in the UK.

Editorial
Hannah Chukwu
Amy Mae Baxter
Adriano Noble

Contracts
Megan Phillips
Amy Patrick
Anne Goddard
Bryony Hall
Sasha Duszynska Lewis

Sales
Caitriona Row
Dominic Smith
Frances Doyle
Hannah Methuen
Lucy Hine
Toluwalope Ayo-Ajala

Design
Nico Taylor

Production
Narges Nojoumi

Copy-Editor
David Bamford

Proofreader
Saxon Bullock

Publicity
Millie Seaward

Marketing
Emily Moran

Operations
Kellie Barnfield
Millie Gibson
Sanjeev Braich